Teaching
the Birds and the Bees
without the Butterflies!

A Stress-Free Guide for Parents on
How to Talk to Young Children about Sex
from a Christian Perspective

By Traci Lester

Dedicated to the love of my life, Chris,
and my four beautiful children
Cici, Boo, Bug, and Banana.

I love you beyond words.

Contents

Preface

"Hey Dad, I know a baby comes out of the mom, but how does it actually get in the mom?" My head shot up. I was fortunate enough to be in the next room preparing supper when I heard this innocent question come from my sweet eight-year-old son.

All movement in my kitchen came to a silent standstill. The spaghetti and meatballs could wait. I didn't dare clank a single pot for fear of missing this golden moment. I waited expectantly, hoping that all of the years I had spent instilling values in him would pay off (my husband, that is).

We should have been prepared for such a moment. This wasn't the first child who cornered us with a difficult question. Twenty seven years of marriage and four children together had given us scores of occasions to wish we had the superpower of invisibility. But since we live in reality, and time travel has yet to be discovered, we came up with another game plan.

The Boy Scouts are on to something.

Be prepared.

Early on in our parenting journey we found that an extremely effective method—and our personal favorite—is to buy some time to get our thoughts together before we answer the question. First, we compliment him on what a wonderful question it is. (I have to admit it usually is a pretty good one.) Then we emphasize how delighted we are that he asked us. (Just between you and me, we aren't really that happy, but we feel it's a good thing to say regardless.)

This time was a little different though. For the past few years I had been offering workshops designed to empower parents with effective ways to discuss the touchy subject of sex with their young children. Because of this, I was certain some of it had rubbed off on my shy husband.

HIM: "*Wow! That is a really good question.*"
ME: Awww…he really is an awesome father!

HIM: "*I am so happy you asked me that.*"
ME: (Sigh.) I think I'm falling in love with that man all over again.

HIM: "*Actually…hmmm…well…let me think.*"
ME: Uh oh, he's losing it. Hold tight, Honey, you can do this!

HIM: "*You know what? Mom actually teaches that for a living. Why don't you and I go ask her.*"

Um, yeah. He did.

Have you ever found yourself in this situation? It's pretty rough, isn't it? I have met very few individuals who are eager to have *The Big Talk* with their children. And, if I'm being completely honest with you, I think those people are kinda weird. (If you are one of these parents, please don't be offended. I'm actually a pretty nice person, and I happen to like weird people.)

The truth is that most of us are terrified of having this conversation with our child. Of course we know it's our responsibility. But let's admit it, we secretly wish someone else would do it while we go shopping. Would you believe that some anxious parents have actually approached me and asked if I would consider giving the sex talk to their kids?

What are they, crazy?!

It sure would be nice to get out of it, wouldn't it? But we are the parents; it's part of the package. We *have to* do things we don't want to do. Diaper blowouts at the grocery store, 104 fevers at 2:00 AM, or sitting through a three-hour-long dance recital for your daughter's one-minute ballet debut. All of these things pale in comparison to the task of talking about sex with your kid.

But I hope after reading this book you will appreciate that, even though it doesn't feel like it, this part of parenting really is a privilege. I think it's even possible that by the time you finish it you may actually look forward to talking about sex with your child.

Too much?

Okay, you may not *ever* look forward to it, but I feel pretty confident that you won't fear it quite so much.

Disclaimers

I'm not a doctor. You will not find a certification on the subject of sex hanging on my wall. Although I'm no sophisticated authority, I am by nature an encourager. (I found that out when I *encouraged* myself to take a personality test.) I am an average teacher, but more than anything I am a really good friend. I pray this book will inspire you to be bold with a subject that causes even the most valiant among us to cower in fear.

If you were seeking a comprehensive book on the subject of sexuality, this *isn't* it. Experts with far more knowledge than myself have written wonderful and thorough books on the psychology, physiology, and theology of sex and sexuality.

This book is a gift from one friend to another. It's designed to be a stress-free, easy-to-follow approach that I hope will be a great resource for you. Through it you will find the support and practical tools to courageously tackle this sensitive subject with your child.

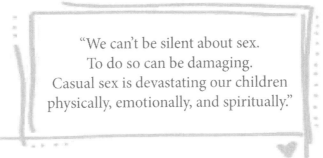

"We can't be silent about sex.
To do so can be damaging.
Casual sex is devastating our children
physically, emotionally, and spiritually."

STATISTICS

• 47% of high school students in the United States have had sexual intercourse.[1]

• In the United States 1 in 4 sexually active teens become infected with an STD every year.[2]

• Although sex is common, most sexually active teens wish they had waited longer to have sex, which suggests that sex is occurring before youths are prepared for its consequences.[3]

In the book *A Chicken's Guide to Talking Turkey to Your Kids about Sex,* authors Kevin Leman and Kathy Flores Bell get right to the point.

"The raw reality of today's society, in which the vast majority of kids have sexual intercourse before the age of twenty, means that a passive approach to parenting will no longer work. If you do what many parents do—cross your fingers, hope for the best and stay silent—your family will add to the statistics of out-of-wedlock pregnancies, sexually transmitted diseases, and broken hearts, all before your children reach the age of twenty one."[4]

All of this sure is discouraging, isn't it? And here I told you I was an encourager.

Read on… I promise it gets better.

part one

The
PARENT
Approach

You did *what*
with Daddy?!
—Emily, age 9

chapter 1

TASHA

For the last twenty years I have served in the pregnancy care ministry. Some days the work at the pregnancy center is remarkable. A young woman walks through the doors scared and confused, and in her desperation contemplates a heartbreaking decision that will have lifelong consequences. Instead, she chooses to give life to her child and we are privileged to have assisted God in a miracle.

But if I'm honest, some days at the pregnancy center are just plain discouraging. And sometimes, I confess, my attitude isn't what it should be.

Tasha, a high school sophomore, arrived at the center at 3:50 p.m., ten minutes before closing time. She came in with two other girls. All were requesting a pregnancy test, and all were *very excited* at the possibility of being pregnant.

"Are you serious?" I thought to myself. "All three of you need a pregnancy test?"

I did a pretty good job hiding my frustration as I had them begin the process of filling out the necessary forms.

Now, this was not the first time a group of teen friends came in together with such a request, but for some reason that day it really bugged me. I was going on my 17th year serving in the ministry, and maybe I was just becoming disillusioned.

As I escorted Tasha back to the bathroom for her urine pregnancy test, I skeptically thought to myself, "This will likely go nowhere." (Sometimes I even surprise myself by my lack of faith.) While I waited for her to return, I said a quick prayer for a better attitude and tried to get myself in check.

Negative.

In ten minutes Tasha had the answer to the question she came in with. She was not pregnant. And there was no mistaking the disappointment in her eyes. My heart slowly began to soften towards her.

What makes a 15-year-old girl want to be a mother? Some young girls see it as a means of keeping the guy, others to prove they are grown up, while most believe a baby is the answer to the unconditional love they are desperately searching for.

Tasha was all of the above.

He used her when he wanted sex and ignored her when he didn't. He didn't love her, but she wanted him to. She used her body to get his love but fell short. A baby would cement the deal, and now even that plan had failed.

"Tasha, can I ask you a question? Please really think about it before you respond, okay?"

She agreed.

"Do you believe that you really deserve to have a guy who truly loves you? Not just one who says he loves you just to get what he wants from you, but a guy who will really cherish and honor you?"

She didn't answer. She didn't have to. The tears spilling down her cheeks said it all.

I wanted her to leave knowing that she was worthy of that kind of love from a man. I went on to explain how beautiful and valuable she was. She didn't need to settle for the players and the users, but instead wait for the one who will make a lifelong commitment to her.

Then she said something that left me speechless. "No one has ever told me this stuff."

Still, I felt I needed to prepare her. "You know, Tasha, it's possible that when we go back into the waiting room one or both of your friends will be pregnant. If that's the case, promise me that you won't feel disappointed it isn't you. Try never to forget that you deserve so much more."

I watched her face as she played out the possibility in her mind. She agreed.

I wasn't so sure.

I was really glad we talked about it because friend #2 eagerly met her at the door with news that she was indeed going to have a baby.

I held my breath as Tasha and I locked eyes.

Hers sparkled.

I couldn't believe it! She smiled as if we shared an unspoken secret. There are moments at the center when God unmistakably moves in the heart of a client, and I am completely humbled by it all. This was one. As I hugged Tasha goodbye, I realized my poor attitude was long gone. I watched the door close behind them and smiled, thankful that I serve a God who could bring glory and honor to Himself in spite of me.

That night I lay in bed with a load of questions heavy on my heart. What was Tasha's home life like? Did she have a close relationship with her parents? Did she even live with them? How soon would the message she heard today become drowned out by the even louder messages in her world? Did I really believe that our little meeting meant that much?

I hoped so.

I prayed so.

Over the course of several years, I have had the honor of speaking to thousands of young people about God's plan for sex and inspiring them to wait to have sex until it is best—when they are married. Have you ever seen the goofball abstinence teacher mocked on primetime TV or in the movies?

Yep, that's me.

I actually find it sad that some adults ridicule what I do. Our culture tends to normalize sexual immorality and scoff at wholesome sexual values. It seems that those who value purity and abstinence are considered weird and old-fashioned. They seriously believe I am wasting my time. They say things like, "Kids are going to do it anyway. You're just being naïve if you really think young people will actually wait to have sex until they are married."

I'm a lot of things, but I'm not naïve.

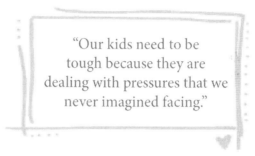

"Our kids need to be tough because they are dealing with pressures that we never imagined facing."

Unfortunately, I see the consequences of sex outside of marriage every day. So they can say whatever they want. That's okay; I'm tough. I can handle it. And you know what? Our kids need to be tough too because they are dealing with pressures that we never imagined facing.

Young people deserve to hear the truth from adults. They are so worth it!

If we are not careful we can easily be brought into the school of thought that sex is no big deal. A good cure for that is to just look around. Our culture is producing more unintended pregnancies, sexually transmitted diseases, sexual addictions, and broken hearts than ever before. I have met way too many teens broken over the poor choices they have made to not try to do something about it.

The message of waiting to have sex until marriage isn't old fashioned. It's a really good message. It is the only way our children can stay 100% sexually safe physically, emotionally, and spiritually.

Still, we have not made the impact we could be making. There is something obvious missing in the whole approach. Teens are having sex outside of marriage at an alarming rate. It troubles me that I would dedicate so much of myself to something that seems to grow in so few of the hearts of the young people who hear it.

Then it occurred to me. What if teens like Tasha had someone consistently reinforcing the message that their sexuality is a precious and priceless gift to be protected? I began to pray for God to give me insight into what was missing.

The answer is **you**.

I wish Tasha woke up each morning to a parent or any loving adult who consistently told her that she is a precious treasure, her sexuality has value, and not to settle for a counterfeit love.

Parents are the key. And the best part of it is that it's not just me saying it, it's the kids. While we parents shake our heads in frustration, resigning ourselves to the idea that we will never compete with the sexual lies the world carelessly throws around, the majority of teens say their parents are the ones who *most* influence their sexual decisions.

Eight in ten teens (80%) say that it would be much easier for teens to delay sexual activity and avoid teen pregnancy if they were able to have more open, honest conversations about these topics with their parents.[5]

Kids want to hear from their parents about sex, love, and relationships. It's very important for parents to understand that they can make a real difference in the choices their children make regarding sex. Yet it can be risky if we put off discussing sex with them until they are fourteen. At that point it may not be possible to totally erase what they have already learned and replace it with what you do want them to know. And if we wait until they are sixteen or seventeen, much of the information they have learned has already shaped their sexual values and parents are left scrambling to do damage control.

Most experts agree that the best time to begin talking to kids about sex is earlier than you might think. You are the best educator for your children, so embrace that role! If you are unsure how to start, the acronym PARENT can guide you.

"If we wait until they are age sixteen or seventeen, much of the information they have learned has already shaped their sexual values and parents are left scrambling to do damage control."

P: PLAN
A: ANTICIPATE
R: RELATIONSHIP
E: EDUCATE
N: NAVIGATE
T: TOOLS

Now, let's regain our confidence and reclaim some lost territory. Be brave—you got this.

I think I'm
gonna be sick.
—Tyler, age 10

chapter 2

"P" IS FOR PLAN

The beautiful sunny September morning was the perfect day to hold the annual fundraising walk for the pregnancy center. After weeks of diligently raising money, hundreds of supporters turned out to walk for a cause close to their heart. This event is an important one to the center, and as a member of the staff I am always so encouraged to see young and old alike come together in assisting young women facing unplanned pregnancies. As they often do, my children accompanied me that morning. I would later regret that decision.

It was set to be a great time for everyone involved—joyful attitudes, smiles all around, generous hearts ready to do something wonderful. The crowd was instructed that the two-mile route was easy to follow. The arrows placed along the route would lead them right back to where they began. The crowd had no reason to doubt the instructions.

They should have.

Because earlier that morning, while volunteers carefully placed each guidepost, my 10-year-old son and his buddy thought it would be a hoot if they followed behind turning the arrows to instead point in random directions.

Imagine hours later when the trusting crowd attempted to follow the confusing directions yet increasingly growing frustrated as the final destination eluded them. While some turned right, others turned left. Most were baffled and left to figure out how to get back on their own.

My son thought it would be funny. It wasn't. (Okay, maybe it's a little funny thirteen years later.) What it really did was just leave everyone feeling very lost.

How about you? Have you ever attempted to follow someone giving direction and about a quarter of the way into the instructions it hits you that the poor things have no earthly idea what they are doing? Bless their hearts.

Even Jesus said it was a bad idea when he told this parable.

Can the blind lead the blind? Will they not both fall into a pit? The student is not above the teacher, but everyone who is fully trained will be like their teacher.
— Luke 6:39 (NIV)

Everyone seems to have a different opinion on the best way to raise children. They even disagree on the subject of sex. I happen to think most of them are confused, yet they are the ones who are screaming the loudest about how it should be done.

"Teens are going to do it anyway. We need to teach them to use condoms or get them on the pill before it's too late."

"Sexual exploration is natural. After all, if it feels good just do it!"

"Sex is no big deal. Everyone is doing it."

"It's okay to have sex as long as you're in love." (Um, hello, the first time I "fell in love" I was nine years old.)

Parents are left to compete against enticing messages, and they often end up feeling alone and lost without direction. Getting your child from point A to point B effectively will be dependent on the quality and clarity of the instructions you give. So what do you do?

You need a plan.

In her lecture *Shaping Your Child's Sexual Values,* Mary Flo Ridley recommends that parents create a mission statement for sex. She encourages parents to ask themselves, "What is it that I want my child to know about sex? There are so many things we *don't* want them to know that we forget that there are the things that we *do* want them to know."[6]

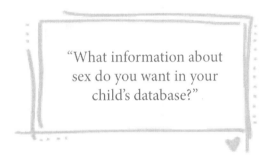

"What information about sex do you want in your child's database?"

What information about sex do you want in your child's database? Before you answer "absolutely nothing," let me assure you that there are some things you want them to know. And although you and I have never met, I think I can guess a few of them.

You want your child to:

- Understand that their sexuality has immense value.
- Realize that choosing to have sex will have consequences for them physically, emotionally, and spiritually.
- Learn how to recognize and protect themselves against people who will harm them.
- Avoid situations that would cause short-term and long-term disappointment and regret.

How am I doing?

It really is best to determine the direction when your child is young to help both of you avoid getting lost along the way. Your job is to make sure your message is clear and that the arrows you set out are beneficial and permanent. It should be well thought out and remain consistent throughout your child's life so you can teach it with unwavering confidence. Because our promiscuous culture has an uncanny way of distorting and blurring the boundary lines of sex, many parents can't distinguish them anymore and have lost sight of what's right and true.

Let me clarify what I'm trying to say by using an illustration I use when speaking to teenagers.

Let's imagine for a moment that I just bought a brand-new smart phone but have no idea how to use it. What should I do? *(It doesn't take them long to advise me to read the instruction manual.)*

"That's right!" I exclaim. "The instruction manual will tell me how it works, what it was designed to do, and how to get the best experience out of my new phone.

Likewise, your sexuality is way too valuable to entrust it to anyone or anything but the one who created sex in the first place. You see, God created sex. He is the greatest inventor ever, and He is the one who wrote the handbook on how to handle our sexuality.

What does He have to say about it?

> *"For this is the will of God, your sanctification; that is, that you abstain from sexual immorality."*
> — I Thessalonians 4:3 (NASB)

When my husband and I established our *plan*, it was important to us that we teach our children that sex is a really good thing; God created it to be good. He created it for pleasure and for the purpose of procreating. But we also wanted them to know that sex is not a game, and although it is a wonderful thing, it should be kept within the boundaries that keep them physically, emotionally, and spiritually healthy and safe. The boundary God established is marriage. He ordained sex, but he also regulated it. And His laws are perfect.

We wanted our children to understand that aside from everything else they will hear about sex: *Sex is a gift from God for a husband and wife to show their love and create a life.*

I remember thinking how cool it was that we actually had a plan. Even cooler? Yep, it rhymes.

This simple sentence serves as a compass for any discussion we have with our children about sex. Whether they are five years old or twenty-five years old, the needle points them in the correct direction. It sets a goal that helps maintain focus and offers us a source of accountability when we face competing distractions in our lives.

When you create your *plan*, consider the things that you think are important for them to know about sex, and then compile those things into one simple statement. Keep in mind that when developing your plan, less is more. Keep it short and easy to understand. Since I am an encourager, I wanted one that was not created out of fear, but rather out of a beautiful vision of things to come.

> *"Where there is no vision the people are unrestrained. But happy is he who keeps the law."*
> — Proverbs 29:18 (NASB)

Do me a favor, and read that verse one more time.

It's obvious that too many people have no vision when it comes to their sexuality, and they have lost their minds in some of the dangerous choices they make. The unrestrained attitude that "anything goes" is leaving a culture of wounded people. And I really believe that if we adults would do a better job casting the beautiful vision for sex, we would see a dramatic change in the hearts, minds, and actions of young people.

Where there is no vision the people are unrestrained. But happy is he who keeps the law.
— Proverbs 29:18 (NASB)

chapter 3

"A" IS FOR ANTICIPATE

*Preach the word; be prepared in season and out of season;
correct, rebuke and encourage—
with great patience and careful instruction.*
— II Timothy 4:2 (NIV)

Forget that! I ain't
never getting married!
— Jeremy, age 10

Ladies, how many times in your life has some guy come up to you with clenched abs and a dare to punch him? Maybe it's just me, but between my two brothers, two sons, and a husband, I kinda feel like it's happened more than I'd like.

Of course, the trick for him not doubling over in pain is that he anticipate the punch. As long as the guy knows it's coming and is prepared for it, he usually can handle a sock from a girl. I've often wondered what would happen if he wasn't ready for it. More than once I've resisted the urge to sucker punch 'em when he wasn't expecting it just to find out.

> *To be Prepared is Half the Victory.*
> — Miguel DeCervantes

There are certain stages in our child's development that we anticipate, and in our expectation we begin preparing for it. Think back to your first pregnancy. You look like the type that isn't going to be taken by surprise. You read all of the expectant parent books, meticulously child proofed your home, purchased the wipe warmer, and deliberated for weeks between the colors Chilled Lemonade and Banana Cream Pie to get just the right shade of yellow for the nursery walls. You did it all in anticipation of the arrival of the newest member of your family.

And what about those Terrible Twos? Whew! Well-meaning friends and family members warn us that they are coming. "Oh, she's a sweetheart now, but just wait until the Terrible Twos!" they sing.

They're right.

The Terrible Twos arrive as expected. Your little cherub quickly discovers the word *no* and begins to challenge you to daily throwdowns like a WWF champ. But since you anticipated it, you prepared yourself in advance, and it maybe didn't seem quite so bad.

One of the best things you can do when it comes to discussing sex and development with your child is to equip yourself for the task. Begin to anticipate the stages of development, prepare for any difficult questions they may ask, and find age-appropriate material that will assist you as you teach them.

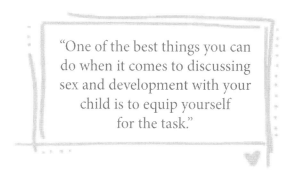

"One of the best things you can do when it comes to discussing sex and development with your child is to equip yourself for the task."

A TIMELINE OF SEX ED

Ages 1-3   Their Body
                  The Differences Between Boys and Girls

Ages 4-7   Pregnancy and Birth

Ages 8-10   Conception and Reproduction

Ages 7-12   Preparing for Puberty

Of course, if we had a way to peek into the future and know when the embarrassing questions will come, it would be much easier to be prepared with a terrific answer. Take it from me, these gems will inevitably come when you least expect it. If your little one hasn't already asked something that takes you off guard, he will. For your personal enjoyment, I have compiled a list of some of my favorite questions from my own children about sex and development. Some of these were asked in the privacy of our home. Others were not.

How did I get out of your tummy?
What does sexy mean?
Why do men have nipples?
(I'm still not 100% sure of the answer to this one.)

Those are kind of cute, huh? But as they got older the questions stopped being cute and started getting tough.

What is rape?
What does it mean to be a virgin?
What is oral sex?

My response to each and every one of them? *"I am so glad you asked me."*

"I AM SO GLAD
YOU ASKED ME"

Right about now you're probably asking yourself, "Is she serious? Glad they asked?! She really does live in La-La Land! What parent could ever be happy to be asked such uncomfortable questions?"

But expressing an enthusiasm and openness to their inquiries is an essential ingredient in the overall message you want to convey. This type of response tells your child that you are available to them and want them to come to you for that information. Questions such as these are asked in complete trust that you will provide the right answer. Even better, it gives you as a loving parent the opportunity to answer it wrapped tightly in *your* values; framed in what is important to you.

On-the-spot interrogations are never fun. If you have ever been to a stressful job interview, you know the importance of having prepared responses. And even though it is nerve wracking, when you anticipate the question, you may be more comfortable in your answer. When you are comfortable, you are confident. When you are confident, it sends the message that you know what you are talking about and can be trusted.

Resist the urge to give your child the brush off. For example, if during breakfast your seven-year-old asks you what *humping* means, try not to choke on your toast and answer with, "That's something we don't talk about...ever! Please just finish your cereal."

> "It gives you as a loving parent the opportunity to answer it wrapped tightly in your values; framed in what is important to you."

Take a moment to gather your thoughts, take a deep breath, and simply answer their question. This is where feeling prepared really comes in handy. (If that example made you throw up a little bit in your mouth, Chapter Five and the Chapter Fifteen have sample dialogues that can help you develop age-appropriate responses.)

Still, children have been known to ambush an unsuspecting parent before they have had a chance to prepare. If you find yourself in this position, simply say something like this.

"That's an important question, and I am so glad you asked me. It's something you learn as you get older, and I really want to give you the best answer. Let me think about that, and let's talk after dinner."

Make sure you do.

If you don't know the answer to their question, you can say something like this.

"That's an interesting question, but I'm not sure. Let's go look it up together."

It doesn't bother your child that you don't know everything. Kids usually are cool with you saying, "I don't know, let's go find out together." It's much better to give that response rather than an inaccurate or short answer given out of panic.

One of my friends told me of a time when her in-laws were visiting from out of state for the holidays. During the hushed candlelit Christmas Eve service, her four year old inquired—at full volume—what *virgin* meant.

If a question is asked at an inopportune moment, there is nothing wrong with letting them know that you will be more than happy to discuss it at a better time.

So, instead of twisting his ear simply whisper in it, *"That's a really great question. I promise when we get home I'll tell you all about it."*

I'm pretty sure my friend didn't hear another word of that evening's sermon. On the bright side, it did give her a little time to formulate a good response.

As difficult as all of this is, it really is a gift to impart truth and values to your child. By creating a comfortable environment of respect and honesty, you open the door for future discussions that will play an integral part in shaping their values.

- Be Bold.
- Be Prepared
- Be Comfortable
- Buy Time if necessary
- Practice!

"Never Let 'Em See You Sweat."
— Dry Idea antiperspirant commercial slogan

chapter 4

"R" IS FOR RELATIONSHIP

Fathers, do not exasperate your children,
so that they will not lose heart.
— Colossians 3:21 (NASB)

Noelle inherited her artistic talent from her daddy. His gift for creating beautiful works of art was only eclipsed by his charm. "Everyone loved my father," she explains. It only took moments in his presence to realize he was a very special man. When the kids in the neighborhood would tease, "My Dad can beat up your Dad!" Noelle confidently responded, "No, *seriously*, mine really can."

"He was perfect in my eyes. To this day, next to God, no one in my life has ever loved me like my father did back then," she says wistfully.

She has very few memories of her parents together. She was four years old when her mom and dad divorced, and he married his soul mate. Noelle's new stepmother explained to her that it was "fate" that they were together.

Noelle didn't even know what fate meant.

For years, she lived next door with her grandparents and the promise that once the storage room was cleaned out, her father would set up a bedroom for her in his tiny house.

It never happened.

Her half-brother was born two years later, and the cluttered room was transformed into a nursery.

He wasn't an everyday kind of dad, but every Sunday, he would load his children into his old '59 Mercedes and head off to church. After Sunday School, he negotiated the same deal that he did each week before. He agreed to buy lunch and take them to a movie, but only after they promised to do the same for him when he got old.

She adored her daddy, and couldn't wait until the day they lived under the same roof. As the years passed, Noelle got older and so did the steady excuses of why it wasn't a good time to move in with them.

The grandfather she was living with got cancer and died the summer between 9th and 10th grade. Her daddy wasn't the same after his father's death. Even when she did finally live with him the bond they shared wasn't the same. They were drifting apart. "Maybe the loss of his father was too painful or maybe he didn't like me having boyfriends, but he began to treat me as if he hated me," she reflects.

Her first sexual experience was within two days of her grandfather's death.

The suspicion that she was sexually active prompted a doctor's visit. That day she left with two prescriptions: one for birth control and the other to treat her newly diagnosed sexually transmitted disease.

"Everyone seemed to be cool with putting me on birth control, so I figured that I had their permission to continue having sex with whomever I wanted."

Still, Noelle didn't always tell the truth when it came to the friends she hung with and the guys she dated. She practiced her father's longstanding motto, "it's always easier to ask for forgiveness than permission." The only problem was that when she did it, she was labeled a liar by him.

She searched for love in each new relationship but ended up just finding sex. "I guess I was just naïve," she says. One Friday night, she and her friend told their parents that they were spending the night with the other. Instead, they hung out with some guys they had just met.

That night, she was raped.

"Devastated, I told myself that the rape was my own fault and wouldn't have happened if I hadn't lied. I knew that if my daddy found out, he would track the guy down and kill him. I just couldn't bear the idea of my father going to jail over something I caused. It was done, and I would never tell."

In 11th grade she wanted a brand-new start, and moved thirty miles away to live with her mother. In the new town she balanced a fast-food job, monthly car payments, and good grades. One weekend she took her father up on his invitation to visit but was greeted with a cold welcome from her stepmother. Noelle was hurt, and they began to argue. "She was really angry with me and followed me outside. She slammed me against my car and called me an ungrateful [expletive.] I refused to fight back because I knew that my daddy would be so furious once he saw the bruises and broken skin from her fingernails on my arm that he would come to my defense."

She was mistaken.

Instead, he looked her in the eyes and said, "The way I see it, you brought it on yourself. There have been a couple of times when I have wanted to do that to you myself. Don't you ever tell me if you are raped or beaten because you will have brought it all on yourself."

"He didn't even know that I had been raped! I felt that I *had* brought it on myself, but I was still *his* daughter. At that moment I can't even tell you what that confrontation did to me. It really changed me."

She was left feeling shattered, betrayed, and unprotected.

In her effort to make things right between the two of them she wrote him a letter. "I'm pretty sure the sheet of notebook paper literally had tear stains all over it. I told him that I was sorry and I just wanted to start over and be daddy's little girl again," she reflects.

"But he said he didn't believe me because I was a liar."

Hurt and angry, she thought to herself, "If you thought I was bad before, *just watch this!* Since he didn't care about me, I didn't care about me. I was going to punish him. I intentionally lowered my standards when choosing friends. All a guy had to do was just tell me that he cared about me and I gave him what I thought he wanted. I can't explain it, but it made me feel good to hurt my dad that way," she remembers.

"At age 18, I got pregnant. That Christmas, my father wouldn't even look at me. I'm sure I was a major disappointment," she says.

Noelle gave birth to a beautiful baby boy who immediately claimed her heart, and a year and a half later a wonderful man proposed to her and her son.

Her dad couldn't make the wedding. It would take many years to mend their fractured relationship.

"In hindsight, I wish he would have had the right words to say or had understood what I was going through. I often wonder if he had said "Noelle you are my child. I want better for you. You don't need to have sex to feel loved because I love you."

"Maybe if he would have said that I would have stopped."

> I often wonder if he had said
> "Noelle you are my child.
> I want better for you. You don't
> need to have sex to feel loved
> because I love you."

For a time we have the ability to put our fingerprints all over our children, especially when they are young. What an opportunity to fashion their hearts and build a relationship unlike any they will ever know. And from the time they enter our world, they study us. They are watching and learning from us when we are completely on our game and even when we are not. Our strengths and imperfections shape them. Although our role as parent is forever, the sad reality is that the further they advance into adulthood, the less pliable they become and the less influence we have over their decisions. We want to get it right from the beginning.

> "If we want our kids to respect our ideas and desire to please us we need to work diligently at building and maintaining that close connection."

The unique bond that unites parent and child assists us in passing on strong values. If we want our kids to respect our ideas and desire to please us, we need to work diligently at building and maintaining that close connection. The open environment and communication that occurs within close families makes it much easier to deal with sensitive issues than those families who are disconnected from each other.

If the *plan* you establish from Chapter Two acts as your compass, then a close *relationship* with your child will be the nourishment to sustain you along the way. Thankfully, when building relationships we have the best tools at our disposable for getting the job done!

- Time
- Communication
- Affirmation
- Touch

TIME

If people knew how hard I worked to achieve my mastery, it wouldn't seem so wonderful at all.
— Michelangelo

Unless you are a genius, things like learning to play a musical instrument or excelling in a sport take a serious commitment of time to master them. At six years old, one of my sons vehemently denied this basic fact. He is a bright boy, but he is certainly no prodigy. One day he convinced himself that, after 15 minutes of strumming his older brother's new guitar, he was qualified to play lead in a band.

We disagreed.

Another afternoon he decided that he wanted to learn karate and convinced me to drive him to the local library for a book on martial arts. Once we arrived home, he tucked the book under his arm and disappeared into his bedroom. An hour later he emerged, clapped the imaginary dust off of his hands, and confidently stated, "Well, one more page and I'm a Black Belt!"

Ha! I just love that kid!

Investing time is essential in building and keeping a strong relationship. We can't just pencil our kids in our calendars when it fits our time table and expect them to feel connected to us. The notion of quality vs. quantity is absurd. Priceless moments with my kids are almost always unplanned. They happen while making school lunches, driving home from school, or pulling weeds. In relationships, without quantity there is not much quality because the opportunities are few and far between. Investing time in them allows you to grow closer to them. You learn to recognize your child's individual character along with their own unique set of strengths and weaknesses.

COMMUNICATION

"No more talking, Sweetheart. Mommy's ears need a rest."

My sweet 10-year-old daughter has just spent the last 25 minutes of the car ride to her doctor's appointment relaying every single moment of her school day.

I have a lot on my mind. If I had to repeat to you everything she has just told me, I couldn't. I'm pretty sure there was something about her friend Savannah throwing her banana away at lunchtime because it was black and disgusting. I think she mentioned needing new flip flops since the weather is getting warmer and her feet are getting bigger. Oh, and apparently she had a bit of invisible lint that was tickling her ankle all day long during class.

Am I a bad mother to tell her to stop talking? I hope not. Realistically, I just don't have it in me to give my children my undivided attention every time they open their mouth to speak.

But most of the time I put a lot of effort into listening to what they have to say. Someone once told me that the key to any great relationship is communication, and listening is a big part of communicating. I may not be able to provide my child total focus rushing through the grocery store to pick up dinner, but I can set my magazine aside for a moment or let him interrupt my favorite television program when he wants to talk to me.

The busyness of life can give kids the impression that we are closed off without intending to be. No guilt trip here— it's just that you may be surprised how often you *don't* stop what you are doing, look them in the eye and really listen when you *do* have the chance. Genuine focus goes a long way when validating how important someone is to you. It sends the message that you are interested in what matters to them.

How did your own parents rate in this area? You probably communicate with your child a lot like they did with you. If you want your child to communicate well with you and the important people in their life, model it. Discussing everyday things, even the things that seem insignificant, will influence how comfortable they will be having conversations about the really big stuff like sex, relationships, and drugs with you.

AFFIRMATION

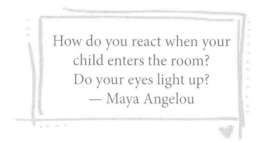

How do you react when your
child enters the room?
Do your eyes light up?
— Maya Angelou

Every child needs at least one adult in their life who believes they are extraordinary. There is something incredibly affirming when you walk into a space and just by being, you move someone with happiness. In an instant, your unique beauty and unlimited value is recognized.

Additionally, we can either build up or we can tear down with our words. The spoken word has an enormous impact on a child's identity and what they believe they can accomplish.

The tongue has the power of life and death.
— Proverbs 18:21 (NIV)

Both genders respond to affirmation, but I am convinced that the male species has an even stronger response when they are validated by others, especially the women in their lives. Try it! Compliment your son on a specific quality that you admire about him, and you will witness it firsthand. As much as they try to be "all cool" about it, they just can't seem to hide how much it means to them that you respect them.

TOUCH

Parental instincts take over within the first moments of a newborn's life. The hectic delivery room activity quickly fades away as blissful parents gently trace perfect ears, grasp miniature fingers, and kiss tiny pink lips. Those early cuddles were the very first form of communication between you and your child. Even as they grow, holding them close continues to validate the trust between you and, interestingly, it often stands alone without the need for words. A caring touch from a parent or trusted adult is the best and fastest way to calm a frightened child or express loving feelings. To simply reassure them verbally without physical contact just doesn't do the trick.

Quite a bit of scientific research has been done on the importance of touch in the development of babies and children. Research by the University of Miami's Touch Research Institute has discovered that human touch has a lot of physical and emotional benefit for people in all age groups. The Institute demonstrated that, among other things, touch lessened pain, increased growth in infants, and improved immune function.[7]

Some children are more affectionate than others, but they all need some form of human touch. Whether it is a pat on his back, a ruffle on her head, or being cuddled on the couch, touch is an integral part of generating closeness between you and your child.

COMMUNICATION, TIME, AFFIRMATION and TOUCH

These four tools are essential for building a strong relationship. Each of them says to your child, "I love being with you. You are important and significant in my eyes."

Consider your relationship with your child a bridge. *Communication, time, affirmation and touch* not only build a great bridge, but also help to maintain it over the years.

When they are toddlers, we just love spending *time* with them and sharing each new experience, don't we? Even on the rare occasion that we forget its importance and attempt to use the bathroom alone, they lovingly remind us through violent pummels and ear piercing screams on the other side of the door.

First words are uttered, then sentences begin to form, and parents delight in the task of teaching new ways of expression through verbal language. *Communicating* with a young child is such a delight!

"Look what big muscles you have; you are so strong!" or "You look like a royal princess in your beautiful pink dress!" Toddlers are attention-seeking missiles and we are oh-so-happy to oblige them. We are their biggest cheerleaders as we *affirm* their every move.

And, oh my, aren't they absolutely adorable? We really can't keep our hands off of them! We instinctively know the importance of *touch* when we playfully scoop them into our arms or protectively grab their hand when crossing the street. We lovingly kiss skinned knees and enjoy bedtime snuggles.

Implementing these tools is just so easy…when they are little.

Then everything changes. One day the stranger walking through the front door startles you until you realize that your delightful angel has transformed into a moody, independent, and sulky prepubescent. Taking a sip of coffee you wonder how long it's been since you used any of the relationship-building tools.

Time? Ha! How can you? They don't even appear to want to be around you. The bedroom is now their preferred living space. When asked if they would like you to accompany them clothes shopping, they affectionately inform you that they'd rather not be seen with you. You now embarrass them.

Communication? Hmmm…don't have too high of expectations at this age. Any communication skills they once had will pretty much regress over the next few years. Aside from the occasional grunt now and then, you won't get a whole lot of one-on-one chats with them unless you really work at it.

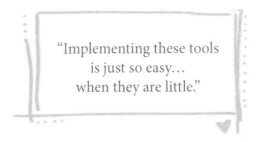

"Implementing these tools
is just so easy...
when they are little."

Affirmation? See...now here's the thing, they are going to become incredibly selfish and extremely lazy. Validation from you becomes more challenging when you find yourself replacing all that sweet talk with a lot of good old-fashioned nagging.

Touch? If they get within reaching distance, I say GO FOR IT!

Puberty looms in the near future and a strong yearning for independence makes using the tools of *time, communication, affirmation, and touch* becomes more challenging. If you take your cues from them, you will begin to pull back and gradually use these tools less and less. It doesn't happen overnight, but one day you may find you and your child are drifting apart. By the time she reaches her teen years, you may be completely disconnected from her.

Fast forward a couple of years. The bridge relationship that was once incredibly strong has been neglected, and is actually beginning to look pretty rickety and unstable.

Then a crisis happens in your teen's life.

Maybe you find out your son got drunk at a party or you found an inappropriate letter from your daughter to her new boyfriend. Perhaps you find evidence that they visited a graphic internet site on their computer. And now it's your job to get across the bridge as fast as you can to save them.

I hope you never find yourself at this point, but I pray if you do, the bridge you labored to construct over the years is sturdy and strong enough to cross over, scoop them up, and race them to a safe place.

They are counting on you to push through the grief they dish out and continue to *communicate* with them, spend *time* with them, *affirm* them, and *touch* them. Because even though they aren't showing it, they still need you to provide these things just as much as they ever have.

> "If you take your cues from them, you will begin to pull back and gradually use these tools less and less."

chapter 5

"E" IS FOR EDUCATE

A little boy had been playing outside with the
neighborhood kids when he came into
the house to ask his grandma a question.

"Grandma, what is it called when two people sleep in the
same room and one is on top of the other?"

Feeling a little taken back, she bravely took a deep breath
and decided just to tell him the truth.
"It's called sexual intercourse, Darling."

Little Travis responded, "Oh, okay,"
and went back outside to play with the other kids.

A few minutes later he came back in and said angrily,
"Grandma, it isn't called sexual intercourse!
It's called BUNK BEDS,
and Jimmy's mom wants to talk to you!"

You shall teach them diligently to your sons
and shall talk of them when you sit in your house
and when you walk by the way and when you
lie down and when you rise up.
— Deuteronomy 6:7 (NASB)

Three weeks after the birth of my first baby I attended a women's Bible study meeting to show her off. The attention my newborn baby girl received was suddenly eclipsed by the arrival of one extremely frazzled mom. Plopping herself in the seat next to me, she painfully announced, "Ugh, I had the talk with Brittany this morning."

A chorus of gasps filled the room. "You did?" a barely audible whisper was heard from somewhere across the room.

Through hands that now appeared permanently affixed to her face came a muffled response impossible to comprehend. But it didn't matter. We understood perfectly.

Silence filled the classroom. We stared at our friend with eyes full of both admiration and sympathy. I had never had the sex talk with my mother, which by the way, was just fine with me.

My gaze slowly left the woman on my right and landed on my three-week-old daughter sleeping peacefully in my arms. I made a silent vow to her then and there that I would *never* put either one of us through the humiliation.

The Big Talk. Those three little words can cause a mother's heart to race violently and a father to break out in an ice cold sweat. But *why* do we fear it so much? Some will say that the reason we experience this anxiety is because we feel embarrassed or uncomfortable chatting about such a deeply intimate issue with our children. However, when interviewing young parents, the unease they experience seems to be more than just a feeling of awkwardness. We are parents for heaven's sake! We are used to being embarrassed. Sure it's an uncomfortable discussion, but I think most of the forestalling comes from the desire to protect our children and keep them innocent for as long as we possibly can. We nobly think that by postponing any discussion about sex until they are older, we will shield them from the harsh reality of life.

The hitch is that if we don't talk with them during their early years, someone else will, and they're going to get it all wrong.

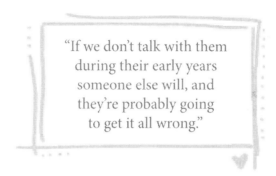

"If we don't talk with them during their early years someone else will, and they're probably going to get it all wrong."

BE THE "EXPERT" ON SEX TO YOUR CHILD

Be a "sexpert." Yep. I said it. Woo Hoo!

Establish yourself as the expert on sex to your child. That's my goal. I want my children to know that anything they want to know about sex, I have the answers (not that creepy kid, Carl, she sits next to on the school bus).

You can earn the title of being the authority on the issue by discussing the value of sex and God's plan for it *early and often* with your child. If you don't, your child will likely think that when he has questions about sex, he will find his answers from the kids in his class or by visiting an internet site.

I promise you can do this, and I want to help you feel more at ease. For now, all I want you to do is relax and take a short walk with me.

"Relax and take a
short walk with me"

C'mon, it'll be fun!

Isn't this nice? Large cotton-like clouds set against the Carolina blue sky. Patches of sunlight create stepping stones along the path ahead. Rows of full-leafed maple trees wave us along in the breeze.

Now, as we stroll along, take note of the different landmarks we approach. Each milestone is placed in a strategic location indicating what lies ahead and will help you understand your child's developmental stages. There will be no unexpected surprises around the corner. On this walk you will learn to recognize occasions to discuss sexuality with your child and establish a foundation of sexual values.

Familiarize yourself with each marker on this trip because **the next time you travel this road, your child will be walking alongside of you.**

Look, we are approaching the first guidepost already!

GUIDEPOST
1

**THEIR BODIES/THE DIFFERENCES
BETWEEN BOYS AND GIRLS (ages 1-3)**

"Head and shoulders, knees and toes, knees and toes." Happy little songs like this help children understand that each part of their body has a name, and are often the very first words they will learn. Teaching the different parts and purposes of the body comes naturally to parents. It begins when they are babies and continues over the next couple of years.

Since they discover their genitalia early on, you might as well take the opportunity to include it in the introductions.

But, let's be honest here. There is an interesting condition that affects many parents. Don't worry, I'm not judging, I was afflicted at one time, too. For the life of me, I could not seem to bring myself to use the correct biological names of *those* body parts.

If you stammer over the word *penis*, then you know exactly what I am talking about! If you're unsure, here's a little quiz. Do you refer to any body part in the diaper/underwear area as a *ding-dong, hoo-ha and/or winkie?* If your answer is yes, then I'm probably referring to you.

While you don't want to sound like you have a PhD in genitalia, you really should use the correct names for body parts. You don't have to use them all of the time, but be bold and occasionally incorporate the words *penis* and *vagina* instead of *thingamajig.* When referring to where the baby grows inside of a woman's body, use the proper terminology *womb* or *uterus* instead of *tummy* or *stomach*.

Kids notice that boys and girls are a made differently, so grab at the chance to teach the differences between boys and girls during these early years. For example, when she asks why her little brother has some strange extra parts during his diaper change, explain how God created boys and girls differently. When changing clothes, she may wonder why Mommy's private area doesn't look the same as hers. Explain how our bodies change as we mature. Handling these conversations in the same straightforward way as you teach every other part of his body helps him to understand that there is nothing shameful or embarrassing about it.

Example One

CHILD: "I saw dad's pee-pee."

YOU: *"You did? I'll bet that you thought it looked a lot different than your penis does. God made it so that as boys grow into men, their bodies change too. Your penis will look like that when you are a grown up."*

Example Two

CHILD: "Andrew told me that a baby is growing inside his mommy's stomach."

YOU: *"Actually, it is way better than that! God designed a woman to have a very special place inside of her body called her womb. It is not her stomach, but it is very close to her tummy. Men don't have a womb because men can't grow a baby inside of them like women can. That is a way that men and women are different."*

Even if you choose not use the words all of the time, they still need to be recognizable as the child matures and subsequent discussions take place over the next few years. Think of this as the beginning of the wonderful story of sex, and these are the main characters. (Hee-Hee.)

The reason you probably don't want to teach them these words is it might backfire on you, and they might opt to use them during Sunday School class. Sweet Mrs. Perkins probably won't think that the word *vagina* is nearly as cool as your child does.

If it makes you feel more comfortable, instruct your child that specific rules go along with knowing these words. Remind them that because these are words for the private area, there are certain places that are acceptable to use them. If they want to use them they should limit it to your home or just around the family for now.

Modesty

Doesn't modesty sound just so yesterday?

It's not.

The introduction of the anatomy opens the door for a progressive lesson on modesty. There is a natural protection that comes along with practicing modesty. Be proactive when they are young to avoid problems later. Emphasize that these are special parts of our bodies to be kept covered and private. Define where their "private area" or "personal area" is so they are very clear as to what you are referring. An easy-to-understand demonstration on the specific area that should remain private is to have your children put on their swimsuits (boys in trunks, girls in one-piece) and tell them that their "personal area" is the part that the swimsuit is covering. Instruct them that no one is to touch this private area unless it is by a doctor or a parent who is giving care.

Remind them that modesty refers to dress, speech, and actions.

The next guidepost is just up the road a bit.

Oooo…and it's a good one.

PREGNANCY AND BIRTH (ages 4-7)

Without sexual intercourse there would be no pregnancy. Thankfully kids don't know this. They will be interested in the concept of birth long before you need to discuss the wonders of conception. A child of five or six is generally mature enough to handle the basic facts of pregnancy and birth.

Have a seat and let's hang out at this marker for a few minutes. This discussion makes you feel a little more uneasy than the last one, doesn't it? You may be comforted to know that if you are observant, you will find lots of illustrations right in your own backyard that will ease you into the pregnancy and birth discussion.

For instance, isn't that your pregnant sister-in-law Susan resting in the shade over there?

"Hey Susan, over here! Wow! Look at the belly on her! How much weight has she gained with this pregnancy, anyway? Shhh…here she comes."

Women like Aunt Susan are great instruments for introducing pregnancy and birth. Your little one observes her Aunt Susan's body changing, which gives you a great illustration for how an unborn baby grows inside of a woman. Maybe your son will get to witness it firsthand when you discover the stray cat he has secretly been feeding for the last two weeks was actually pregnant and gives birth to six crying kittens under your front porch.

The point is, as they start observing this in their own environment, they may begin to inquire about how it all works. Simply answer any questions that they bring up. If they don't ask, lovingly initiate a conversation with them as opportunities arise. (This is when the names of those body parts will come in handy.)

YOU: *"Aunt Susan is going to have a baby!" A tiny baby is growing inside of her womb and will soon be ready to come out and be your cousin."*

If he continues to ask questions, answer them!

CHILD: "How will it come out?"

YOU: *"Wow! That is a really good question. I have been waiting until just the right time to tell you, and since you are asking me that must mean you are ready to know! Do you remember how a baby only grows inside of the mother's womb? During this time the baby isn't ready to live outside of his mommy's body. He gets his food and everything he needs, to grow bigger through the umbilical cord attached to his tummy. Do you see your belly button? That is where your umbilical cord used to be. When a baby starts growing, he is so tiny that only a microscope can see him. But he grows very quickly and after nine months he is ready to come out. When that time comes, the baby sends the mommy's body a special signal, and the mom goes into labor. Labor means work because it is a lot of work for the mommy to get a baby out. Strong muscles around her womb tighten, and those muscles push the baby from the womb/uterus, through the birth canal, and out of the special opening between the mother's legs called the vagina."*

Since not all babies are born this way—and you will want to cover all of your bases—you may opt to include a brief discussion on caesarean sections.

"Most babies are born this way, but sometimes it is too difficult for a baby to go through the birth canal. The good thing is that the doctors and nurses know when this happens and will make a special opening right below the belly button. It is called a caesarean section or

c-section. Your sister was actually born this way!"

Now, as your friend I feel it is only fair to warn you that *The Big Talk* guidepost is up the road and around the bend. Just as we used Aunt Susan as a great illustration to lay this foundation, continue to be attentive to your surroundings and recognize ways you can reinforce the idea of conception. Do you see those pears growing on that tree? Great lesson on how God designed every seed to reproduce after its own kind (Genesis 1:11). See that acorn that fell from the oak tree over there? That's another perfect occasion to demonstrate the cycle of reproduction.

And just look those dogs playing in that field... Oh my, are they doing what I think they are doing?

Um...well okay...another teachable moment, I guess.

GUIDEPOST 3

THE BIG SEX TALK (ages 8-10)

We've finally arrived! *The Big Talk!*

Hey, wait a minute! Where'd you go? Come back! Trust me, it'll be fine.

By the time your child is between the ages of 8-10 you will have given her the groundwork she needs to understand sexual intercourse. The timing of when to have this discussion is for you to think about. Evaluate your child's maturity level, what they have been exposed to, and what you think they already know. But never assume that your child doesn't know anything about sex just because they are not asking questions.

In the book, *"How to Talk to Your Child about Sex,"* Linda and Richard Eyre recommend age eight as a great age to discuss sexual intercourse. "Most eight year olds are trusting, open, innocent, anxious to please and fairly fascinated by the world around them. They simply haven't yet learned to be embarrassed, sarcastic or cynical." "Regardless of how much they have or haven't heard, whatever is written on their slate is written pretty lightly and can be erased, or rewritten or corrected by a prepared, committed parent."[8]

When they do ask a difficult question, answer truthfully while keeping it simple. Let your child's questions be your guide on the amount of information you give. Start by defining what they already know so you will avoid unnecessarily over-explaining.

HER: "What does sexy mean?"
RESPONSE: *"Great question! Tell me, what do you think sexy means?"*

For the young child, simple is better. You can always add to your answer, but it isn't easy to erase something you wish you hadn't said. Trust me, I've tried.

I began this book with my own personal experience. My thoughtful husband passed our son off to me for this part of the talk. Well, here was "our" response:

"God designed a husband and wife to make a baby together. Since a baby is both a part of the daddy and of the mommy, they need to hold each other very close and their bodies fit together in just the right way. That is how a baby begins to grow inside of the mommy."

We made sure to incorporate our *plan*. Since you want to reinforce that sex is to be kept within the boundaries of marriage as scripture teaches, then include God, husband and wife in your explanation.

A simple response like that may be just what your child needs. He may respond with an, "Okay." and run off perfectly happy with that new information. Not my son. Oh no, he wanted more!

HIM: "But how does the daddy get his part inside of the mommy?"

This is the difficult part because this information might be a little unsettling for them (and for you). But I was feeling exceptionally fearless that day, and I felt he was ready. So I said something like this:

"Good question! This is something you learn as you get older, and I definitely think that now you are old enough to know it. Sex is the special way that God designed a husband and wife to show how much they love each other and make a baby. A baby is both a part of the daddy and of the mommy. The part of the husband is a tiny seed called the sperm, and the wife's part is a tiny egg called the ovum. Since the two parts are in two different bodies, they need to join together some-how! The husband and wife have to get really close and use their pri-

vate parts in order for that to happen. The husband puts his penis inside of the wife's vagina. The tiny sperm comes out of him, and it swims to the ovum inside of the wife's body. Once the sperm and ovum join together a brand new life has begun: half of the mommy and half of the daddy to make one beautiful new person!"

HIM: "Really? That. Is. So. Disgusting."

That's okay. Here's the thing: I want him to think sex is gross right now. For a kid, it is gross. At age eight his body doesn't have the level of sexual hormones that gives him the desire for sex. Soon enough, he will quit thinking how gross it is, and it will be another set of challenges. I reassured him that when the time comes, I'm pretty sure he will want it.

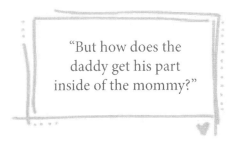

"But how does the daddy get his part inside of the mommy?"

ME: *"I know it seems gross and I don't expect you to understand everything right now, but it is the way God designed a husband and a wife to show their love to each other and to participate in creating life. As you grow older, your body will begin to change. When that happens, you will not think sex is disgusting."*

Now let's imagine for a moment that you are hanging out at this guidepost just kind of chilling on the bench, waiting patiently for your child to start asking questions. You and your spouse are armed with great material, you are psyched and ready, but they just aren't asking anything.

Instead of counting on your child's questions to be the open door for a discussion, you just need to get a little creative, that's all.

Set a date and plan a special time for the event. If you want, you can let them know that you are planning a special grown-up time to spend together. Let them choose their favorite activity, restaurant, etc. You may find the library or your local bookstore has material that can act as a discussion guide for you or may be something they choose to read when they are alone.

"Catherine, you are growing into such a beautiful person! We love you so much, and we are very excited to have this special time with you. We wanted to spend our time having fun and also talk to you about some grown up things that you learn as you get older. You were too young to know these things last year, but this year you are definitely old enough to learn them. God is so good to us! When God created people, he thought it was such a wonderful thing that he also wanted husbands and wives to know the special feeling of creating a person. Do you know how a baby begins? We have a special book to help you understand how a husband and a wife can start a baby and the awesome way it grows inside of the mother."

Adults sometimes get overly stressed about the sex discussion because they mistakenly believe that in order to teach their child they have to tell *everything* they know about sex—the good, the bad, and the ugly! You may be thinking, "I can't tell my child *that*!" You don't have to. They wouldn't understand most of it anyway. At this age make it easy on yourself and just stick with the biology of it all.

"Developmentally birth through about age 10 children cannot understand the concepts of the dangers and pleasures of sexual intercourse. It's great to know that you can take those off the table. What's left is understanding just the biology of it"
— Mary Flo Ridley[9]

Uh Oh! Do you see those ominous black clouds off in the distance? A storm is rolling in. Stick with me. It's going to get a little bumpy.

GUIDEPOST 4

PREPARE FOR PUBERTY

Do everyone in your family a really big favor and prepare your child with good information on some of the changes and challenges up ahead as they approach puberty. Let your child know that as they grow older their bodies will change…a lot. In short, hormones will mess them up for awhile. Their physical, emotional, and social life will be affected. If you wait to discuss this with them in the midst of the chaos and turmoil it may not go over so well. Begin preparing them ahead of time. Maybe even take them out for another special evening or weekend. Reassure them that although their feelings toward you may change, it is a natural and normal part of growing up. You can make a commitment to each other that you will do everything you can to maintain a loving connection.

YOU: *"Rebecca, do you remember when I told you that as your body changes into a young woman your moods and emotions might change too? Your feelings will feel so much stronger than before. One minute you may feel happy and the other minute sad. It's also very normal for you not to feel as close to me as you did before. You are one of my favorite people, and I don't want us to lose our closeness. Do you think you and I can spend some time together?"*

PUBERTY (ages 8-14)

Ah, sweet puberty, the most turbulent milestone of them all!

Pay no attention to the hazard signs stuck in the middle of road. They were probably put there by some prankster parents who have already traveled Puberty Road.

Puberty is the time when sex makes more sense to your kid than it did when he was younger. Now is when they can understand the dangers and pleasures of sex. As sexual hormones create an attraction to the opposite sex, they become less interested in the biology of sex and much more interested in relationships. The attraction they feel is an intense feeling and can often get confused with the feeling of being in love. Be the loving influence at this difficult time in your child's life and paint a successful picture that the transition into their teen years will turn out well for both of you. Although puberty can be difficult, it is survivable.

DON'T FORGET THE SUNSCREEN!

I have a friend who is a true believer in sunscreen. She wasn't always. She considered it extremely overrated. That is, until she allowed her beautiful blonde-haired, blue-eyed toddler to spend a few hours at the beach without it. An afternoon spent splashing in the cool waves and building sandcastles resulted in one very miserable, blistered child that evening.

Parents find themselves spending a lot of time slathering the thick cream all over their children in an effort to protect tender skin against painful sunburn. It also serves as a precautionary step against the damaging long-term effects of harsh sun exposure.

Likewise, instilling Godly values regarding sex is like saturating your child's heart with a layer of protection against a permissive sexual culture. It's not that they won't feel some heat when exposed to the things that contradict your values, but with the protection it offers they'll be less likely to get burned and suffer future harm.

So, when you walk along the path with your child, don't forget your values. **Apply generously and reapply as necessary**.

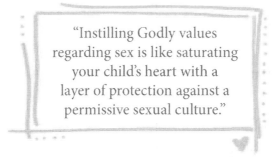

"Instilling Godly values regarding sex is like saturating your child's heart with a layer of protection against a permissive sexual culture."

Mom, do you think
Dad has ever had sex?
— Jackson, age 7

chapter 6

"N" IS FOR NAVIGATE

Trust in the LORD with all your heart
and lean not on your own understanding;
in all your ways submit to him,
and he will make your paths straight.
— Proverbs 3:5-6 (NIV)

I've come to a conclusion. My GPS can either be my best friend or my worst enemy. She could either be an accommodating and supportive travel companion or a sadistic tour guide riding in my front seat, and I'm not sure when I get in my car which one she will be. She has led me flawlessly to my hairdresser's house on the smallest of country roads. On the other hand, she has deceptively guided my family to a state park in the beautiful mountains of North Carolina only to leave us on a deserted cul-de-sac. She left us staring at each other in total confusion while somewhere in the background she confidently declared "You have now reached your destination."

I can't always trust her. She does not navigate well.

To navigate is to take action. It means to direct carefully and safely; to plot the path and position; to find a way through a place or direct the course of something (someone in this case).

We are entrusted with the task of guiding our children on their path from birth to adulthood. Easing some of the bumps in the road requires us to note any obstacles that might deter from the values we seek to establish. Although the barriers are challenging and frustrating, learning to identify them will enable you to equip yourself and your family with tools to navigate around them.

IDENTIFYING POTENTIAL OBSTACLES

The Influence of the Media

If you choose *not* talk to your child about sex, the entertainment industry is probably where they will get most of their information about it. The campaign to win your child's heart is launched through seductive movies, explicit music and magazines, crude television shows, and the ever-available internet. Our permissive culture has turned sex into a game; a way to get what you want from someone else. Using, abusing, and reusing sex is the constant theme and it permeates their world. Media exposure is virtually inescapable yet it has a hefty influence on how our kids shape their view of sex. The media whispers into the ear of your child, "Your sexuality has no value." The most heartbreaking thing of it all is that too many of them believe that lie.

> "The media whispers into the ear of your child, "Your sexuality has no value."
>
> "The most heartbreaking thing of it all is that too many of them believe that lie."

To expect anyone to escape unscathed from the level of exposure of a completely flawed message is a delusion. In fact, studies show that 12 to 14 year-olds with high exposure to sexual content in the media are 2.2 times more likely to be sexually active than those who are not.[10]

Peer Pressure

If all of your friends jumped off of a bridge would you jump too? I heard that question countless times growing up from all of the adults attempting to school me on the negative effects of peer pressure. The thing is, I'm pretty sure there were times growing up that if everyone in my group were jumping off of a cliff, I really may have too!

The desire to fit in is exceptionally strong for kids. It may not be much of a big deal before age six, but beginning around third grade, the longing to be accepted by their peer group begins to take shape and quickly intensifies. Balancing the right things they have been taught and still look cool to their friends can be difficult. At age eight it's hard not to cave into the kid pushing him to steal a piece of candy from the class treasure box. At age fifteen, the pressure to drink alcohol, smoke cigarettes, or experiment with sex may seem almost impossible to stand against.

The Desire to Date

"Two little lovers sitting in a tree K.I.S.S.I.N.G.
First comes love, then comes marriage,
then comes baby in a baby carriage."

Somewhere along the line we got this all mixed up, didn't we? Kids want to start dating earlier than ever before. Before mom and dad concede and give in to their request to have a boyfriend or girlfriend, let's think about it for a minute. What is the purpose of dating? It's to find a future husband or wife. I realize that may sound very old school to some, but when we allow children to date someone, break up, quickly find someone else, and break up again, it teaches them to use others to satisfy their needs. Once they cease to make you happy, just move on!

Sounds more like a lesson on divorce.

Children shouldn't be in exclusive relationships *period*. Dating leads to kissing, kissing leads to petting, and petting leads to sex. Then sex can lead to many other issues like broken hearts, unintended pregnancy, sexually transmitted infections, etc.

Yet, isn't it so adorable when your five-year-old son has a crush on the darling brown-eyed girl in his kindergarten class? It is just so incredibly sweet that you may even catch yourself encouraging his newfound love interest.

"Hey Grandma, did you know that Stevie has a new girlfriend?" you tease. "He's in love, aren't you, Stevie?" Poor Stevie is left completely bewildered by the entire conversation.

A girl of eight may ask, "Mommy, can I have a boyfriend?" Generally, this amounts to nothing more than just declaring to the world—or just Mrs. Arnold's 3rd grade class— that the two of them are an item. The problem is, if you allow it at age eight, she may be left feeling confused when she asks at age twelve and receives a firm "no way" from you.

CBS News asked a group of middle school students if they thought twelve years old was too young to start dating. "The general consensus from the kids in the group was that age twelve seemed to be a good age to begin dating. But dating means different things to different people. One student described dating this way, "Some people just hang out with their boyfriend or girlfriend. They hug them and kiss them. But some people get sexual about it."[11]

Age twelve is too young to date. Just sayin'.

NAVIGATE THE OBSTACLES

I'm not a gambler (but I've been told by extended family members that I need to be careful because I do carry the gene). Anyway, if I was a gambler I'd wager that you take great precautions to protect the things that are most precious to you. Whether it's your father's rare coin collection or your grandmother's antique locket, you take careful steps to ensure that those cherished things remain safe from anything that might damage them.

Of all your treasured possessions your child is the most valuable.

If you determine your family is facing an obstacle/pressure, you will need to navigate your child safely through or around it. Generally, this is done by placing a boundary or limit specific to the situation.

I once heard someone say that it would be so much easier if kids would just note the obstacles for themselves and make responsible choices as adults do. Seriously, that person hasn't met some of the wacky adults that I hang out with. Why do we expect our kids to act like adults? They are kids, preteens, and then teenagers, but they are *not* adults. Their brains are still under construction and will continue to be until they reach adulthood. For now, they don't rationalize and make decisions as mature adults do. So parents and trusted adults need to stand in the gap and help them make responsible decisions.

If you spot a potential problem down the road you can redirect your course by setting a boundary. For instance, if your child is at risk for being exposed to sexually explicit things on the internet, you can limit what sites they have access to by setting parental controls. If they are hanging out with someone who you know is a bad influence, don't allow her to spend time alone with that particular friend.

Sometimes you don't identify an obstacle until (Ba-Bam!) you crash right into it. For instance, you may be watching your favorite television program during family hour and an inappropriate scene comes out of nowhere. At this point it would be impossible to avoid this obstacle, so simply climb over it by seizing the moment and taking the opportunity to discuss it with your child.

YOU: *"This show kind of portrays sex like it is no big deal, doesn't it? I know Mary and Brad are really attracted to each other, but do you think they are really in love? What do you think about the fact that they just met yesterday and are already having sex?"*

Staying the course and navigating your child through the mess will help protect them from potentially disastrous consequences later.

Staying the course and navigating your child through the mess will help protect them from potentially disastrous consequences later.

I found that tides and currents do not determine destination.
That is what rudders and engines and sails are for.
— Russ Metcalfe

Aren't you glad you only
had to do that once?
— Devin, only child, age 9

chapter 7

"T" IS FOR TOOLS

We may not be able to prepare the future for our children,
but we can at least prepare our children for the future.
— Franklin D. Roosevelt

The Massai tribe of East Africa certainly has a unique way of ushering their young boys into adulthood. Among the many rituals and customs within the Massai culture, the lion hunt is one that is held in high regard among its people. Pursuing and killing a male lion while armed with only a spear and a sword is a symbolic rite of passage for a young Massai warrior. The hunt allows the boy an opportunity to demonstrate bravery and show off his fighting ability. To return with a slain lion brings honor to the young man's family and is a sign of great personal achievement.[12]

Wow! I'm just excited when mine feeds his hamster without being reminded.

Unleashing a gang of teens loose into the wilds of Africa carrying a couple of lame weapons for protection sure doesn't seem to be much of a defense against the king of the jungle.

I can just imagine the nervous father attempting to prepare the boy the night before the hunt.

"So, Bundi, tomorrow you become a man! The lion hunt begins at sunrise. Are you prepared?"

"Uh, I guess so."

"You shined your shield, right? Did you sharpen your spear, Bundi? You really should have a sharp spear."

"Yeah, it's pretty good."

"Sit up straight, Bundi! You are a warrior for goodness sake! You got any questions?"

"Umm, well, I guess I was just kind of wondering...um...how fast can a male lion run anyway?"

"See! Now, that's a good one! From what I remember, pretty fast! And since you consistently seem to receive low marks in speed and endur-

ance class, I want you to stay close to that little kid, Koomie. His legs are short and your mom and I are pretty sure you can outrun him."

It's comforting to know that most of us will never release our off-spring into the untamed jungle of Africa. Even so, they still face some very real dangers in the world. The temptation to rebel and participate in at-risk behaviors like sexual promiscuity, drug experimentation, and binge drinking is still a very real threat.

Parents cannot be ever-present to ensure their children steer clear of temptations and pressure. However, we can be proactive and provide the tools and training to avoid or escape risky situations. By practicing good decision making skills through role play and refusal skills in advance, even very young children will gain the confidence needed to resist peer pressure when they are away from you.

Start children off on the way they should go,
and even when they are old they will not turn from it.
— Proverbs 22:6 (NIV)

ROLE PLAYING

It is to our advantage that very young children love to imitate, learn and play with us. The possibilities are endless when we choose to use role playing to reinforce strong values. The next time you play, grab a Barbie or a plastic dinosaur—whatever your kid is into right now— and get creative. During silly play time, make it count and weave a lesson on values into it!

YOU: *"I need your help, Superman! My friend and I are at the store, and he's telling me to put the pack of gum into my pocket and take it out of the store without paying for it. What should I do?"*

CHILD: "No, You can't do that! That is stealing!"

YOU: *"Oh, thank you, Superman! I didn't know what to do because I didn't want my friend to be mad at me and stop liking me."*

What you just did there was prepare them in case they are pressured to do something they know is wrong. It reinforces their values, and it teaches them that being the hero is cool.

Here's another example:

YOU: *"Barbie, that man over there is asking us to go with him to help him look for his puppy. Should we go with him?"*

CHILD: "Yes! Let's go help him!"

YOU: *"But wait! My mommy says I should never go with a stranger unless I ask her first. Hasn't your mom told you that, Barbie?"*

CHILD: (Realizing she wasn't thinking) "Oh…yeah."

YOU: *"Hurry! Let's go tell our moms."*

This will also help you see what your child already knows, identify if you have overlooked teaching them something, and indicate how they might respond if ever placed in a similar situation.

The best way to deal with peer pressure is to simply avoid it in the first place. But haven't we all found ourselves in an intense pressure situation when we felt that we were in way over our heads and knew we needed to get out?

Older children may be concerned about hurting their friends or peers feelings by not engaging in an activity they know they should not do. They may be afraid of losing a close friend or being teased by the group. As the U.S. Department of Health and Human Services suggests, give them a N.I.C.E way out of it by teaching and practicing excellent refusal skills. [13]

The N.I.C.E. Refusal

N: Say, "NO," not "maybe" or "later." Your child will begin to recognize when and how to say no as you establish boundaries with them *before* they are confronted with the pressure. When the time comes, they will be prepared for it.

I: Follow with an "I" statement. This will give the person pressuring them their own reason for not wanting to engage in the situation. For example, "I don't want to get caught." "I don't want to get into trouble." "I am not allowed to do that." "I don't feel like it."

C: CHANGE. Teach your children to change the topic or even the location. "Did you do your homework today?" "Are you going to the game tonight?" or "C'mon let's just go to Ashley's house." "Let's get out of here."

E: If these strategies do not help, your child needs an EXIT plan. They should leave the situation immediately.

Remind them that they can always count on you to help get them out of any situation. If they need a ride home, tell them to call you immediately and say they are not feeling good. (This is true. If they are getting pressured to do something they know they shouldn't do, then they *aren't* feeling very well.)

If they need you to come and get them because they are in a bad spot they can always text you privately. If that's not possible and they need to call you, they can save face in front of their friends and still get the cryptic message to you that they are in trouble. Establish a prearranged code phrase like "Is that Fido barking?" which means come pick me up now!

A few weeks after settling in our new home near Charlotte, North Carolina, we set off to visit the site of the first documented discovery of gold in the United States: The Reed Gold Mine in Cabarrus County, North Carolina. John Reed served in the Revolutionary War. He was an illiterate German soldier who deserted into the backwoods of North Carolina and became a humble farmer. One Sunday afternoon John's 12-year-old son, Connor, went fishing and returned with a large shiny yellow rock. It was perfect! After all, they needed a doorstop and it was just the right size. The 17-pound gold nugget sat propping a door open for the next three years. When he finally got a clue, John took it to a jeweler. Very interested in purchasing the rock, the jeweler told John to just name his price. He returned home with a whopping $3.50, *one-tenth of one percent of its true value.*[14]

Oh, that crazy John! He just didn't realize the value. Had he known, he would have never let it go for such a cheap price. The family would have treated it much differently.

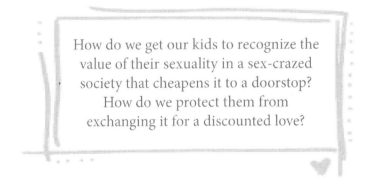

How do we get our kids to recognize the value of their sexuality in a sex-crazed society that cheapens it to a doorstop? How do we protect them from exchanging it for a discounted love?

They would have placed it in a safe place and protected it until it was the right time to redeem it. If he had identified its true worth, he would have understood that they were all in possession of something marvelous.

How do we get our kids to recognize the value of their sexuality in a sex-crazed society that cheapens it to a doorstop? How do we protect them from exchanging it for a discounted love?

By giving them a beautiful vision for their sexuality and equipping them with good tools (refusal skills, wonderful role models, and books/magazines/music that align with your values) will help them keep temptation in check.

I can still remember when we gave our oldest daughter a special gift to remind her of the significance of her sexuality. On her thirteenth birthday she slipped it on her finger and hasn't taken it off for the last twelve years. The tiny heart enfolded in a delicate bow is easy to miss. Although there are no words inscribed on or inside of it, it says something truly beautiful. The gold ring reminds her that her sexuality has value, that she is worth waiting for, and that the real thing is out there waiting for her.

"We need parents to offer us more. We need to know that something beautiful and better exists. We need to understand that it is possible to discover romance at its best. We need to meet the Author of romance. He can script our story in His perfect way and teach us to love like He loves. Faithfulness begins long before we ever meet our spouse. This generation is hungry for "something better." When parents pass on a vision of how romantic and fulfilling God's version of love can be, young people whole-heartedly embrace this higher standard."
— Eric and Leslie Ludy[15]

Seriously?
— Samantha, age 12

chapter 8

SEX AND FIRE

I watch him intently. While aunts and uncles, cousins and grandparents are lost in the laughter and conversation of the evening, I can't take my eyes off of him. His shameless campaign ended when we elected to allow our 13-year-old son the sole responsibility of building and tending the campfire. I wondered if anyone else appreciated that the magnificent heap of intertwined sticks and crunchy orange leaves took him two hours to stockpile earlier that morning.

After carefully constructing a precise tower, he reaches for the lighter, and in a click, a tiny flame starts low and quickly ignites the smaller twigs. He moves with an ease that surprises me, and I realize he is so much like his father and older brother.

He pokes and stirs. He crouches and stands. When it flares, I tense.

He doesn't.

When it's subdued, I relax a little. He takes his eyes off of his masterpiece long enough to notice me staring at him.

We smile at each other.

When he walks over to me and asks, "Mama, would you like me to roast your marshmallow?" I almost lose it.

Years ago, Chris and the kids constructed the fire pit out of large rocks that they heaved up from the very same woods it borders. I am trusting my son to keep the flames contained within the small circle. To lose control could create an inferno that would threaten to consume everything I cherish most.

Darkness begins to quiet the guests. Weary little children sprawl themselves across the laps of their parents and voices begin to speak in hushes. Dancing flames and steady crackles mesmerize us all. The fire continues to illuminate the night and provide warmth from the chilly autumn air. I am happy.

I hope my son's choices about sex will be as carefully chosen as the material he selected to build the fire. I pray he maintains control and realizes his choices can either produce potentially damaging consequences or something truly wonderful. Just like the contained fire, I want all of my children to realize that the beauty of sex is best represented when kept within the boundaries God intended—marriage.

The mediocre teacher tells. The good teacher explains.
The superior teacher demonstrates.
The great teacher inspires.
— William Arthur Ward

part two

Implementing
The
PARENT
Approach

chapter 9

DEVELOP YOUR PLAN

DEVELOP YOUR PLAN

List the things that you want your child to know about sex.

What values do you hope your child carries into his/her teen and adult years regarding sex?

What was the best/worst message you received regarding sex when you were growing up?

Reflecting on your own parents and how they did or did not handle the issue of sex, which things would you like to avoid or imitate?

Write a simple sentence or two that captures your values and what you want your child to know regarding sex? Include your favorite scripture on the subject as your basis for this foundation. Remember to consult with the child's other parent so that you are both in agreement with the ultimate message you will give your child. Be clear and avoid a mixed message or negative messages, but rather focus on laying out a clear, positive plan.

chapter 10

ANTICIPATE THE
TOUGH STUFF

ANTICIPATE THE TOUGH STUFF

By what age do you hope to have laid a strong foundation of sexual values for your child?

List any questions that make you uneasy or you feel unprepared to answer should your child ask.

Take the time to formulate appropriate answers in response to the questions you recorded above. (If you need some ideas, see Chapter Fifteen.)

Do you have well-written material about development, puberty and sex in your home that aligns with your values? List the ones you intend to use.

chapter 11

BUILD AND MAINTAIN THE RELATIONSHIP BRIDGE

IDEAS FOR GREAT COMMUNICATION

The Rose and Thorn game is a fun way to elicit conversation and discover the best thing of the day (rose) and the worst thing of the day (thorn) of each family member.

Designate a special place/chair in your home for sharing an especially good or bad day. Make it a safe place where they can discuss anything important to them without distractions.

Maybe your child expresses feelings or questions better in writing. Buy a blank journal and allow them to write a question or thought to leave on your bed pillow. Respond with your answer or thoughts and place back on their pillow. This may end up being a cherished keepsake one day.

Practice Good Listening Skills

Focus on the child. Stop whatever you are doing and thinking about and keep focused on what your child is saying. Remove any distractions like the TV or computer. If they are talking to you from another room, make them come into the same room you are.

Encourage your child to continue sharing by giving him validating messages, such as looking directly at him, getting down at eye level, nodding, etc.

Ask good questions. Avoid questions that require a yes or no response. Instead of asking, "Did you have a good day?" You may want to say something like, "Tell me what the best part of your day was today."

Clarify to make sure that you understand exactly what is being said. Using the term *It sounds like…*is a great way to accomplish this. ("It sounds like you are uncomfortable being around kids who tease other kids, is that right?") Ask necessary questions to understand the situation better. Use the phrase *Tell me more about…* to elicit more information.

Wait until your child has concluded what he is saying before you begin to think about your response. Make sure you have a complete picture of what your child is telling you before you intervene.

You don't have to agree with everything your child says, but speak with encouragement and respect. (I appreciate that you shared that with me.)

Try not to interrupt your child just to speed along the conversation or inject your opinion too soon. Pay attention to body language and facial expressions.

IDEAS TO GIVE AFFIRMATION

Say I love you often.

Give your child a special nickname.

Let them hear you share with others how special you think they are. *"Grandpa, did you know that Heather is such a thoughtful sister? Today, she helped Samantha clean her room and put away her clothes without being asked."*

Highlight their unique qualities. Be specific on what is special about them. Avoid saying things like *"You are a good boy."* Rather say, *"I was so impressed with how you protected Tina from Jacob's teasing when she spilled her milk at lunch."*

Learn what their current favorite song is and consider downloading it on your own device. (You couldn't wipe the smile off of my son's face when he walked into the room and I was listening to *his* song at that moment.)

Ask your child how you can pray for them. Praying with and for them will show that you care about their struggles, and it will increase their faith as well.

TOUCH

Even if you don't have a touchy-feely child, look for opportunities to have physical contact. A cuddle on the couch while watching a movie, wrestling with him on the carpet for fifteen minutes or tucking her in bed each night are wonderful opportunities to display affection.

chapter 12

EDUCATE-
THINGS TO INCLUDE
IN THE BIG TALK

THINGS TO INCLUDE IN THE BIG TALK

Explain That Sex is a Private Subject

"Daniel, because sex is such a private thing, we are not to watch sex when it comes on the television or anywhere else. Also, when we talk about sex it should probably be done with mom or dad until you get older. It is important to allow your friend's parents to have the special talk with them, so you are not to tell them what you know about sex. Jacob's parents would not be happy with you if you told him about sex before they have the chance to teach him."

Discuss How the World Views Sex

"Because you have been taught about sex, you will be seeing and hearing a lot about it. Since we live in a broken world, most of what you hear will be all messed up. You will probably hear things about sex that go against what we have taught you. You may hear people talk about sex in a dirty way or use bad words to talk about it. Usually when you hear people use bad words they are just trying to be cool. They don't realize that God gave it as a special gift between a husband and wife even though a lot of people have sex without being married. It's sad that so many people are using it in the wrong way."

"When you hear things about sex that go against what we have taught you, just think to yourself, **I know the truth.**

Reassure Them That You Will Always be Willing to Talk With Them About Sex

"If you ever hear something that you aren't sure about let us know, and we will always give you the correct answer. Also, let us know if anyone is asking you questions or giving you information about sex that just doesn't sound right."

chapter 13

NAVIGATE THE OBSTACLES

NAVIGATE THE OBSTACLES

Make a list of the things that consist of your child's everyday world (e.g., school, sports teams, favorite shows, Girl Scouts, baseball, etc.)

Looking over your list, are there things that could present a potential obstacle to your *plan*? If so, how can you place a boundary or limit to avoid it?

Friends

Encourage your child to develop friendships with those whose values are similar to their own. Explain to them that this will help them avoid pressure to do something they don't feel good about.

Make your house teen-friendly. Get to know your child's friends and determine any pressures they might be experiencing through those relationships.

Ask your child questions about their close friends. Good questions asked in a calm manner will allow you to think the situation through and decide if this child really is a good friend. At this point, don't judge, just get the facts.

Make sure you know where your child is hanging out. If he/she is spending a lot of time at a particular friend's house, make sure you are comfortable with the environment.

If you are concerned about a particular child, ask other adults. Talk to other parents, counselors, teachers or coaches who know the child. Do they have any concerns?

Monitor closely. Stay in contact with your child and know where they are at all times.

Watch for any red flags your child may exhibit since spending time with a friend (slipping grades, bad language, more defiant attitude, etc.). If you have any concerns, share them with your child.

Intervene when serious issues emerge. If the friend is clearly a bad influence, it is time to stop the relationship.

Dating

No Early Dating. Studies show that young people who start dating early are more likely to become sexually involved at an earlier age.

Determine the age your child can begin dating. Make it clear that your child will not date anyone more than two years older or younger than he/she is.

Encourage group activities.

Do not allow a member of the opposite sex over when parents are absent.

Do not allow your child to entertain a member of the opposite sex in personal spaces like bedrooms.

Media

Know what your kids are watching, reading, and listening to. Try to get interested and share it together. While affirming your child's interest you can also monitor them. If the material is inappropriate, turn it off.

Monitor what you are watching around them. Be an example to them of what is acceptable to watch and listen to.

Inappropriate situations in the media are almost unavoidable. If you find yourself faced with one, seize the moment by discussing the unsuitable situation.

Internet/Social Media

Before allowing them to set up an online account, you can choose to write out a family contract with your guidelines.

Get a parental filter for your computer. If you feel your child is not trustworthy, you will need to monitor them more closely.

Keep an eye on their pages to monitor their activity. When they are younger, you should know their password. As they grow older, they may view that as an invasion of privacy. As long as they have not given you any reason to distrust them, you may want to allow them their privacy. Know who they are following and who is following them on social media sites.

Sit down together and establish the family rules. Explain to them that no personal information like phone numbers or addresses is to be shared without your permission. Make sure that they know they are not allowed to follow people they do not know.

Explain that they need to be very careful about what they post. Once it is online, you cannot erase it and it will be there forever. Colleges and prospective employers check out their applicants on social networking sites. Most kids don't understand this concept of long-term consequences so reinforce it often.

Ask if it's okay to follow them. If they prefer that you don't, respect that. You can still monitor them by knowing their password and checking it occasionally or if a concern arises. If they are okay with you being their "friend," they will probably make you promise them that you won't post on their wall!

If they are spending a lot of time at their computer yet their website does not reflect it, they may have set up an alternate account to avoid you seeing their activity.

Set time limits on when they can use the computer (e.g., between 4:00 p.m.-5:00 p.m. and 7:00 p.m.-8:00 p.m.).

It all just sounds
so wrong.
— Aubrey, age 10

chapter 14

UTILIZE GREAT TOOLS

UTILIZE GREAT TOOLS

Model healthy sexuality in your home. Even when they act grossed out when you give your spouse a smooch or have a romantic evening cuddled on the couch, there is something very secure when a child knows that their parents deeply love each other. Alternatively, not only would it be a hypocritical message if your child discovers his dad views pornography but it can also make a damaging imprint on their heart. If you are a single parent, carry yourself with integrity and avoid setting any double standards in your own dating life.

Take some time and search out books, magazines, and movies that align with your values. Little girls will especially love the story of the *Princess and the Kiss* by Jennie Bishop. The story tells of a princess whose loving parents give her "a kiss" right after she is born. They inform her that this special kiss is a gift from God, and she is instructed to "keep or give away as she sees fit." Though many potential suitors come in the hopes of acquiring her kiss, she holds onto it until the one comes who is worthy to receive it.[16]

While your daughter or son may become slightly more embarrassed to talk about sensitive issues as they grow older, a handpicked, well-placed age appropriate book or magazine that just happens to be lying around the house will generally peak her interest and intrigue her enough to sneak it to her room to read it privately.

If you keep your eyes peeled, you may even find a popular athlete or famous celebrity who publicly states their commitment to abstinence until marriage. These gems are the darlings of parents everywhere. They will reinforce your point and give you some street cred.

Even before they can pronounce the term *Accountability Partner* you should facilitate play dates with children whose family shares your values. Friendships that bloom as young children may continue on for years and be a source of strength for each of them.

Peer pressure can go either way. It can be a very positive thing when children share strong morals and watch out for each other.

Even though we wish we could follow them around to ensure they make good decisions we just can't. (I can't count how many times my 25-year-old daughter has reminded me of that.) Provide them the tools to get out of a difficult situation and practice role playing and refusal skills. Teaching these tools will strengthen your child's independence and help them develop an inner discipline when faced with temptation or unwelcome pressure.

If a purity ring isn't appropriate, consider your child's unique personality and get creative. A Bible, necklace, wristwatch, keychain, or pocket knife can be a cherished keepsake.

The Three Most Powerful Tools

Trust in the Lord with all your heart and lean not on your own understanding, In all your ways submit to Him and he will make your paths straight.
— Proverbs 3:5-6 (NIV)

Sooner or later parents realize that we are not in control of everything. Although there are limits on what we as parents can do, God is limitless. For the Christian, you possess the *most powerful weapons ever created* in the fight over your child's heart and mind.

Prayer

Pray for your child's protection, that their thoughts will be pure, they avoid tempting situations, and for strength when they are weak.

Do not be anxious about anything, but in every situation, by prayer and petition, with thanksgiving, present your requests to God.
— Philippians 4:6 (NIV)

The Bible
Seek out God's Word for guidance.

Your word is a lamp for my feet, a light on my path.
— Psalm 119:105 (NIV)

Holy Spirit
Rely on the Holy Spirit for wisdom and discernment.

But the Helper, the Holy Spirit, whom the Father will send in my name, will teach you all things and remind you of everything that I have told you.
— John 14:26 (NIV)

chapter 15

Q&A

Q&A

Sample dialogues included just because I like you. Feel free to take them word for word, mix 'em up, or go completely rogue. Remember to keep the tone as casual as any other conversation.

What is a penis?
The question may come after you explain to your daughter that boys and girls are built differently and have different special parts or maybe she heard the term from someone else.

"That's the special private part that only boys have. Just like you have a vagina, they have a penis. It looks different than a vagina, but it is still just as private. Do you remember what private means? We cover it with our underwear. No one is to pull down your underwear, and no one is to touch that area except for someone who helping you clean or a doctor is examining you."

What is a vagina?
"That's the special private part that only girls have. Just like you have a penis, they have a vagina. It looks different than a penis, but it is still just as private. Do you remember what private means? We cover it with our underwear. No one is to pull down your underwear, and no one is to touch that area except for someone who helping you clean or a doctor is examining you."

What if I catch my young child playing doctor with another child?
This is scary to parents because we know the damaging effects of sexual abuse. For the very young child, you can take comfort in the fact that, although it is unsettling as a parent, it is also common and normal. It's likely there is nothing sexual in the exploration and is almost always just a natural curiosity. If you catch your child or hear that your child has participated in this activity, the first thing to do is to take a long deep breath. Don't freak out. Your reaction should be calm because you don't want to scare or shame them.

"Hey Sweetheart, I want to talk to you about what happened today. First of all, I know that you are probably really curious and interested

in what other people's bodies look like. I realize that I haven't told you (or recently reminded you) of something very important. Do you remember what your personal area is? We don't touch people in their personal area, and we don't allow people to touch our personal areas either. If a friend ever asks you to, I want you to tell me. Nothing is a secret between us. If you want to know things, you need to ask me. It's my job to help you understand things."

If you ever catch your child in this situation, I think it is wise to let the other parent know what happened and how you handled it. If you are concerned about the behavior repeating with that particular friend, don't be afraid to set boundaries.

If you are at all concerned that it was abnormal behavior (more explicit) than things the typical child should know, it could indicate sexual abuse or exposure to explicit behavior (something they saw on TV, etc.).

Should I bathe with my child?
Through ages one to three, bathing together is beneficial as long as you are comfortable. Great teachable moments and easily explained ideas can occur during bath time. For instance, how a man's body or woman's body changes and grows as they get older, and why it looks different than their own.

Every family is different. There are conflicting opinions out there on nudity in the home. I would say that once you begin feeling uncomfortable, it is probably time to establish boundaries. About the ages four and five, accidental exposure will likely happen and just become another teachable moment. By age five, a child is able to bathe himself with your supervision and little assistance.

How can I teach my child modesty?
"Tyler, today I heard Johnny talking to you about his private parts. Some of the words that he said sounded silly, didn't they? I suppose he thinks it's funny, and he gets a lot of attention when he talks like that. But I don't want you to. Just as we cover those private parts of our bodies, we also don't talk about them outside of our home either."

"Julia, isn't it wonderful how God created our bodies to work so perfectly and look so pretty? All of our body is wonderful, but not all of it should be shown to others. We respect our bodies and cover certain parts to protect ourselves."

"Grace, I know it seems that the girls who wear the most revealing clothes are often the ones who get the most attention. All girls like attention from guys. The problem is that even though they are getting the guys to pay them attention, they are losing something too. Guys and girls are so different from each other. When a guy sees a girl dressed sexy, he may think of her as someone he would like to have sex with and not think of her other special qualities. I wonder if she even realizes the seductive message she is sending."

How do babies get out of the mommy?
"Even though a baby is very comfortable and warm inside of the mommy, the time comes when it is big enough to come out and be loved on by her family. Women have a special opening between their legs called a vagina, and the baby is born through this opening."

If your child is a girl you hopefully have already discussed this part of her body. If your child is a boy, this is a simple answer that he may be content with. For the particularly inquisitive child, you can discuss it more in depth.

"When that time comes for the baby to be born, the baby sends *the mommy's body a special signal and the mommy goes into labor." Labor means work because it is a lot of work for the mommy to push her baby out. Muscles around the womb tighten, and those muscles push the baby out of the uterus, through the birth canal, and out of the special opening between the mother's legs called the vagina."*

What if they are not asking any questions?
Sorry, it's inevitable. You *will* have to have the sex talk. Plan a special time with them (a day at the park, a weekend getaway, an evening fishing on the lake) and go for it.

Should the parent the same gender as the child be the one to have the talk?

If it is a planned discussion, it makes it easier to decide who will lead it. Each family is unique. Since no two are exactly alike, consider each parent's set of strengths and their comfort level. Both mother and father should be prepared to answer unexpected questions because we can't always plan when our kids will ask them. If they are comfortable, it is ideal that the parent of the same gender discusses the technical part. If your child is comfortable, both parents should take part so your child can get both the male and female perspectives.

For single parents—like most everything else—the responsibility falls on you. The content is the same.

What is sex?

"Sex is the special way that God designed a husband and wife to show how much love each other and make a baby. A baby is both a part of the daddy and of the mommy. A tiny seed called the sperm is the part of the husband and the wife's part is a tiny egg called the ovum. The sperm and the ovum have to join together. Since the two parts are in two different bodies, the husband and wife have to get really close and use their private parts in order for that to happen. The husband puts his penis inside of the wife's vagina. The sperm leaves the husband's body through his penis, and it swims to the ovum inside of the wife's body. Once the sperm and ovum join together a brand new life has begun—half of the mommy and half of the daddy to make one beautiful new person!"

How can I start talking about puberty?

Girls generally begin between ages 8-13 and boys between the ages of 10-15. Prepare your child for what to expect and how their body and emotions will change, and comfort them that the changes they will experience are very normal.

If your daughter is around 8 years old and you haven't already had this discussion with her, you will definitely want to prepare her once you see any breast development. Your pediatrician should be able to tell you when puberty is close. Menstruation usually starts about 1-1 ½ years after breast buds appear. Provide her with a discreet period kit (pad, cleansing wipes, etc.) to keep with her so that when it happens it doesn't frighten her, and she knows exactly what to do if you are not present.

"Jenny, you are growing up so fast! I have noticed that your body is even starting to change. Have you noticed too? You are beginning the process of changing into a young woman called puberty. Boys and girls both go through puberty, but everyone goes through it at different ages. Most girls go through it between the ages 8-13. It really is an exciting time, but the changes can be difficult sometimes. You may feel confused about what is happening. I can remember when I went through puberty. I had so many questions! I had heard so many things from the other girls and didn't know whom to believe. I wish my mom had talked to me about what to expect so it would have been easier to go through the changes."

"Mark, I can't believe it! Every time I look at you, you look stronger and taller than before. I have noticed your body is changing into a young man, which means that you are going through puberty. All boys and girls go through puberty, but everyone does it at different ages. Boys generally go through puberty between ages 10-15, so that makes you right on time! You may already know some of these things, but I want to make sure that you know what to expect and how your body will change. I was about your age when I went through puberty. Everything seemed to change so quickly! It wasn't just my body but my emotions too. I seemed to get sad or mad easily. I felt really good one moment and really bad the next. I had so many questions, and I'm glad my parents prepared me for what to expect. They assured me that what I was going through was normal and made it so much easier for me to deal with all the changes. I hope you feel comfortable enough to ask me anything."

What about Wet Dreams?
"Because your body is growing into a young man it is making more sperm than before. When it has made too much you may ejaculate in your sleep. Other than being a little messy, it is completely normal and

really no big deal. Some boys might wake up and not know what happened. They may think they wet the bed and be really embarrassed. I just want to prepare you in case that ever happens."

What if I don't know the answer to their question?

Simply admit that you don't know the answer and look it up together.

"That is such a good question! You are thinking of things I haven't even thought of yet. I'm not sure what the answer is to that one. Let's go find out together."

"Hmmm…let me think about that one for a little while. Can I get back to you on that?" (Make sure you do it.)

How can I teach my child about sexual abuse?

YOU: *"You know today I was thinking about how much I love you and want to protect you. You are special to so many people who love you. When we love someone, we show them in all different ways. We do nice things for them, we say nice things to them, and we touch them in a nice way. What are some nice touches?"*

THEM: "Hugs, kisses, holding me close when I'm scared at night."

YOU: *"Those are good touches, aren't they? What if someone hits, pushes, or pinches you? What kind of touch would you call that?"*

THEM: "A bad touch."

YOU: *"Very good answer! Some adults, like mommy and a doctor need to sometimes touch you in your personal area. We do that to provide care, like when we are helping you clean yourself or when you have a checkup. If someone else ever wants to touch you in your personal area, that's called a secret touch, and a secret touch is a bad touch. If someone ever wants to give you a secret touch, I need you to tell me. Never keep it a secret. Always tell me if someone has touched you in a secret way or in a way that made you feel yucky, okay?"*

What if my child has been exposed to pornography?
This is a difficult one. When children view explicit material, they simply can't "unsee" it. If you find your child has been on a pornographic internet site or has seen images in a magazine or other source, try not to react in a condemning way. If you shame them they may put up a wall between the two of you. So, how you approach them is very important. Here are some questions to ask that you will need to know:

1. Did they initiate the internet search or did they come across it accidentally? They may be curious about things, and you can reinforce that this is not the way to learn about sex as it can be dangerous and addictive.

2. Who exposed them to it? This will help you identify those in your child's life who may be a poor influence. One of my children told me about a kid on the school bus who accessed porn on their smart phone and showed it to her. Ugh!

3. What exactly did they see?

"Jacob, I want you to know that I love you so much. I thought you should know that I found out that you were on an internet site that had inappropriate pictures. Before you think that I am angry with you, I am not. I am not happy that it happened, and I want to tell you why, okay? I understand that right now you are very curious about sex; that's very normal. Pictures and videos of sex are called pornography. The problem with looking to pornography for answers to your questions is that you will get the wrong ones. Sex is special and pornography takes all the specialness away. You might have come across it by accident, but you shouldn't try to see it. Pornography can be dangerous and addictive. I want you to come to me with your questions, and I will always be honest with you."

What if my young child asks what an abortion is?
"Most mommies are really happy that a baby is growing inside of her. But sometimes a woman may get pregnant and be so scared that she decides she doesn't want to be a mommy. There is a place she can go

where they take the little baby out of her womb before it is big enough to live in the world. Because it wasn't ready to come out, it stops living. Abortion is a very sad thing and goes against God's plan because he loves the baby growing inside of the mommy very much." (Jeremiah 1:5; Psalm 139:13-16)

How do I discuss homosexuality with my child?

Kids often use the term gay to describe something as lame or stupid. They may hear someone being called gay and wonder what it means. If they ask you directly or you happen to hear them using this term, you can say something like this:

"Did you hear Jack use the word gay today? It made me wonder if you even know what that word means. Some people use the term gay when they are actually trying to say that something is stupid. That is wrong and hurtful to do. Gay actually means something else, anyway. Being gay is when two women or two men have chosen to love each other in the way God created a man and a woman to love each other. It is also called homosexuality. The Bible says that homosexuality is not God's plan for us, and it is a sin. God hates sin, but he loves all people. We should never make fun of someone who is gay, but instead we should pray for them to come to follow God's law." (Romans 1:26-27; 1 Corinthians 6:9; 1 Timothy 1:10)

What if I catch my child masturbating?

Very early on, children learn that it feels good when they touch their private parts. Although this is very normal, it can sure make adults uncomfortable! One day you are enjoying your favorite movie and look over to realize that your four-year-old son is enjoying his favorite thing. We don't have to sit and pretend it isn't happening right next to us. The first thing you can do is try to redirect him/her. If they are persistent—and some are very persistent—you can say something like this.

"Sarah, if you are going to touch your private area, you need to find a private place to do it. It is not polite to do that around others. I wish you wouldn't do it because I like having you with me, but if you keep doing it, you will need to go to your bedroom."

As your son or daughter approaches puberty, you may accidentally discover them practicing this behavior. Give your child an extra measure of sensitivity on this because of the embarrassment factor. The last thing they want to do is discuss with their parents what they are doing behind closed doors. Their private world is sacred ground and, if we enter it, it should be done very lovingly.

Regardless of your thoughts on this sensitive matter, the fact is that this is an almost universal behavior, especially among boys. Because the Bible is quiet on the subject of masturbation, it is a controversial subject among many Christians. Seek out respected teachers and leaders that address the topic of masturbation and its consequences and decide how you might handle the issue with your child.

What if we have an out of wedlock pregnancy in the family?
I would take your child's lead on questions about this. If they begin to question how Aunt Ashley is pregnant but isn't married, here is a way to handle it:

"God's plan is for babies to be born to mommies and daddies that are married because they made a promise to be together forever. That is always the best way to bring a baby into the world. Still, it's possible to make a baby even when you are not married, but it is not the way God planned it. God's Word tells us that each life is very precious to Him, and we will love this baby very much because it is a special part of our family".

If your child is more mature, continue to affirm the truth of God's Word. Consider this an opportunity to display and extend love and understanding to another and affirm the sanctity of human life.

"God's Word tells us that only those who are married should have sex. He established this boundary to keep us safe and loved. Some people disobey God in this area and choose to have sex anyway. Since having sex sometimes makes a baby, some babies are born to mothers and fathers who are not married. It is always best for a baby to be born to parents who have promised to stay together forever. God also tells us in the Bible that he has a special plan for each life, and it should be

protected and loved inside and outside of the womb. We will love this baby very much because it is a part of our family."

You may choose to bring the conversation you had with your child to the attention of Aunt Ashley just in case your daughter corners her next Thanksgiving with a new set of questions.

What about my own past?

It is possible to be truthful with our children without confessing all of our deep, dark secrets to them. It's not for them to carry. Your biggest concern is probably being perceived as a hypocrite. If you have made past mistakes, you know how painful they can be. This is motivation for helping them avoid repeating them. Your young child will probably not ask you this question, but your preteen or teen might. Consider your child's personality and maturity level as this will determine how they handle the information. The *You-Did-It-So-Why-Can't-I* child might use it as leverage against you while others might learn from it. If your child does ask you point blank if you had waited and you feel they are mature enough, you can respond with something like this:

"I love you very much, and I want to be honest with you. I really wish I had known all of the things that you do. Unfortunately some things I had to learn the hard way. That is why it is so important to me to share the truth about sex with you. Even though it's difficult to share these things with you, you are worth it for me to be honest with you. My past mistakes are something that I hope you learn from, but your future choices are what really matter. I pray every day that you will be much stronger than I was at your age."

What if my child walks in when we are having sex?

Three words: Lock that door! Teach your child as soon as they are able to understand, they need to always knock on a closed door. If it does happen, depending on their age, their reaction will vary. It may be upsetting to a child to see their parents having sex. It can look like their parents are hurting each other. Simply stop what you are doing. (It's okay, at this point, you'll probably want to!) Calmly go to your child to reassure them.

"You know that Mommy and Daddy love each other very much. Sometimes we show our love by holding each other really close. That's the special way God designed married people to show how much they love each other. They just want to feel really close when they are alone. Mommy and Daddy need our private time, so it's important that you always knock on our door when it is closed. We love you and will always be there when you need us. Let me tuck you back into bed."

Couldn't I just let the school teach my child about sex?

I just hate when my child complains, *"My teacher doesn't do it that way!"* That's because the teacher probably got to them before I did. As frustrating as it is, I can handle it for long division and fractions, but I don't want to hear it regarding sex. Keep your expert hat on! Give accurate information on sex with Godly values attached to it before they are introduced to it by a teacher.

The unfortunate fact is that most schools are teaching sex because most parents are not. Schools generally have some development and sex education built into their curriculum.

The school will make this information available to you when requested. If you feel comfortable after researching the material and the values align with your own, you can use it as a springboard for discussing it with your preteen.

"I've been meaning to ask you how the sex ed classes went today at school. Were you uncomfortable? Did the kids in class act goofy or were they mature about it? Did they discuss anything you didn't know? Do you think most of the kids already knew the information?"

What happens if I have already waited too long?

Be honest and transparent with your child. If they are older and you have not taught them the things you want them to know about sex, just admit it and dive in.

"I just finished reading an interesting book. It made me realize that I may have dropped the ball in teaching you some really important things you need to know. I love you very much, and I need to apolo-

gize. You are probably hearing a lot about sex, and since I didn't prepare you for it, you may have questions about what is true and what isn't. I don't want to embarrass you, but I love you too much not to give you the right information that you need to know and should have been taught in the first place."

How can I feel more confident?

We tend to feel more confident doing something once we do it at all. When you begin to discuss sex with your child, you will feel more confident and you and your child will be more comfortable. Don't let the fear of the conversation prevent you from actually doing it.

What if I find out that my teen has already had sex?

Sadly, I have seen parents pour their heart and soul into the teaching of virtuous values only to have a child reject their training. Although it is not within our power to control another individual, parents still despair and question where they went wrong. If they are under age, place firm boundaries and seek help. They need to know they can have a fresh start and can find forgiveness. Redemption and forgiveness are such beautiful gifts to impart and receive.

Remember your child's value is not in the choices they make. They have innate value simply because they are created in the image of God and deeply loved by Him. Ultimately the choice is theirs. You don't have to agree with them to unconditionally love them. I have seen teens who have made poor choices with devastating consequences yet became incredible walking testimonies of God's grace.

These conversations are only examples to assist you in discussing sex with your child. If you have any questions or concerns, consult your physician or clergy.

SCRIPTURE REFERENCES

Flee from sexual immorality. All other sins a person commits are outside the body, but whoever sins sexually, sins against their own body. — 1 Corinthians 6:18 (NIV)

But among you there must not be even a hint of sexual immorality, or of any kind of impurity, or of greed, because these are improper for God's holy people.
— Ephesians 5:3 (NIV)

And the man and his wife were both naked and were not ashamed.
— Genesis 2:25 (NASB)

For this reason a man will leave his father and mother and be united to his wife, and the two will become one flesh.
— Ephesians 5:31(NIV)

But since sexual immorality is occurring, each man should have sexual relations with his own wife, and each woman with her own husband. The husband should fulfill his marital duty to his wife, and likewise the wife to her husband.
— 1 Corinthians 7:2-3 (NIV)

END NOTES

1 Henry J. Kaiser Family Foundation, "Sexual Health of Adolescents and Young Adults in the United States," The Henry J. Kaiser Family Foundation, March 28, 2013, http://kff.org/womens-health-policy/fact-sheet/sexual-health-of-adolescents-and-young-adults-in-the-united-states/ (accessed December 23, 2013).

2 Alan Guttmacher Institute (AGI), *Sex and America's Teenagers* (New York: AGI, 1994), 149.

3 National Campaign to Prevent Teen Pregnancy, *With One Voice 2002: America's Adults and Teens Sound Off about Teen Pregnancy* (Washington, D.C.: The National Campaign to Prevent Teen Pregnancy, 2002), 2.

4 Kevin Lehman and Kathy Flores Bell, *A Chicken's Guide to Talking Turkey with Your Kids about Sex* (New York: Harper Collins Publishing, 2009), 17.

5 Bill Albert, *With One Voice 2010: America's Adults and Teens Sound Off about Teen Pregnancy* (Washington, D.C.: The National Campaign to Prevent Teen and Unplanned Pregnancy, 2010), 5.

6 Mary Flo Ridley, *Shaping Your Child's Sexual Character*, 2005, Just Say Yes, Compact disc.

7 University of Miami Touch Research Institute, "Research at TRI: General Information About TRI Research," *Touch Research Institute*, http://www6.miami.edu/touch-research/research.html (accessed December 26, 2013).

8 Linda Eyre and Richard Eyre, *How to Talk to Your Child about Sex: It's Best to Start Early, But It's Never Too Late--A Step-By-Step Guide for Every Age* (New York: St. Martins Press, 1999), 52.

9 Mary Flo Ridley, *Shaping Your Child's Sexual Character*.

10 Jane D. Brown *et. al.*, "Sexy Media Matter: Exposure to Sexual Content in Music, Movies, Television and Magazines Predicts Black and White Adolescents' Sexual Behavior," *Pediatrics* 117, no. 4 (2006): 1018, http://pediatrics.aappublications.org/content/117/4/1018.full.pdf+html (accessed December 26, 2013).

11 CBS News, "Is 12 Too Young to Start Dating?" CBS News, May 26, 2010, http://www.cbsnews.com/news/is-12-too-young-to-start-dating/ (accessed December 26, 2013).

12 Justin Cripes, "Becoming a Man Maasai Style Involves Slaying a Lion," *Goshen News*, March 20, 2011.

13 U.S. Department of Health and Human Services, *Parents, Speak Up!: A Guide for Discussing Relationships and Waiting to Have Sex* (Washington, D.C.: U.S. Department of Health and Human Services, 2007), 9, http://talking2teens.utahcounty.gov/_includes/PDFs/Parents_Speak_Up.pdf (accessed December 26, 2013).

14 North Carolina Historic Sites, "Reed Gold Mine: The History of John Reed's Goldmine," *North Carolina Historic Sites,* http://www.nchistoricsites.org/Reed/history.htm (accessed December 26, 2013).

15 Eric Ludy and Leslie Ludy, "Giving your Teens a Vision for Sex: How to Raise Christian-Minded Teens in a Sex-Saturated Culture," *Pure Intimacy*, http://www.pureintimacy.org/g/giving-your-teens-a-vision-for-sex/ (accessed December 26, 2013).

16 Jennie Bishop and Preston McDaniel, *The Princess and the Kiss: A Story of God's Gift of Purity* (Anderson, IN: Warner Press, 1999).

BIBLIOGRAPHY

Alan Guttmacher Institute (AGI). *Sex and America's Teenagers.* New York: AGI, 1994.

Albert, Bill. *With One Voice 2010: America's Adults and Teens Sound Off about Teen Pregnancy.* Washington, D.C.: The National Campaign to Prevent Teen and Unplanned Pregnancy, 2010.

Bishop, Jennie and Preston McDaniel. *The Princess and the Kiss: A Story of God's Gift of Purity.* Anderson, IN: Warner Press, 1999.

Brown, Jane D., Kelly Ladin L'Engle, Carol J. Pardun, Guang Guo, Kristin Kenneavy, and Christine Jackson. "Sexy Media Matter: Exposure to Sexual Content in Music, Movies, Television and Magazines Predicts Black and White Adolescents' Sexual Behavior." *Pediatrics* 117, no. 4 (2006): 1018-1027. http://pediatrics.aappublications.org/content/117/4/1018.full.pdf+html (accessed December 26, 2013).

CBS News. "Is 12 Too Young to Start Dating?" CBS News. May 26, 2010. http://www.cbsnews.com/news/is-12-too-young-to-start-dating/ (accessed December 26, 2013).

Cripes, Justin. "Becoming a Man Maasai Style Involves Slaying a Lion." *Goshen News.* March 20, 2011.

Eyre, Linda and Richard Eyre. *How to Talk to Your Child about Sex: It's Best to Start Early, But It's Never Too Late-- A Step-By-Step Guide for Every Age.* New York: St. Martins Press, 1999.

Grunbaum, Jo Anne, Laura Kann, Steve Kinchen, James Ross, Joseph Hawkins, Richard Lowry, William A. Harris, Tim McManus, David Chyen, and Janet Collins. "Youth Risk Behavior Surveillance Summary --- United States, 2003." *MMWR: Morbidity and Mortality Weekly Report,* 53 no. SS-2 (May 21, 2004): 1-96.

Hamilton, Brady E., Joyce A. Martin, and Stephanie Ventura. "Births: Preliminary Data for 2009." *National Vital Statistics Reports* 59, no 3. Atlanta: National Center for Health Statistics, 2010.

Henry J. Kaiser Family Foundation. "Sexual Health of Adolescents and Young Adults in the United States." *The Henry J. Kaiser Family Foundation.* March 28, 2013. http://kff.org/womens-health-policy/fact-sheet/sexual-health-of-adolescents-and-young-adults-in-the-united-states/ (accessed December 23, 2013).

Lehman, Kevin and Kathy Flores Bell. *A Chicken's Guide to Talking Turkey with Your Kids about Sex.* New York: Harper Collins Publishing, 2009.

Ludy, Eric and Leslie Ludy. "Giving your Teens a Vision for Sex: How to Raise Christian-Minded Teens in a Sex-Saturated Culture." *Pure Intimacy.* http://www.pureintimacy.org/g/giving-your-teens-a-vision-for-sex/ (accessed December 26, 2013).

National Campaign to Prevent Teen Pregnancy. *With One Voice 2002: America's Adults and Teens Sound Off about Teen Pregnancy.* Washington, D.C.: The National Campaign to Prevent Teen Pregnancy, 2002.

North Carolina Historic Sites. "Reed Gold Mine: The History of John Reed's Goldmine." *North Carolina Historic Sites.* http://www.nchistoricsites.org/Reed/history.htm (accessed December 26, 2013).

Ridley, Mary Flo. *Shaping Your Child's Sexual Character.* 2005. Just Say Yes. Compact disc.

University of Miami Touch Research Institute. "Research at TRI: General Information About TRI Research." *Touch Research Institute.* http://www6.miami.edu/touch-research/research.html (accessed December 26, 2013).

U.S. Department of Health and Human Services. *Parents, Speak Up!: A Guide for Discussing Relationships and Waiting to Have Sex.* Washington, D.C.: U.S. Department of Health and Human Services, 2007. http://talking2teens.utahcounty.gov/_includes/PDFs/Parents_Speak_Up.pdf (accessed December 26, 2013).

Twenty Random Facts about the Author

1. My name is Traci Yester-Lester.

2. I was on the TV show Romper Room when I was five years old.

3. I choose the checkout lines at the grocery store based on the scanning speed of the cashier.

4. I have had the privilege of encouraging thousands of young people to honor the beautiful gift of sexuality that God has given them. I just love those kids!

5. I've met the legendary actor Sidney Poitier.

6. I have an organized house but a messy purse.

7. I wish I could appreciate poetry, but honestly most of the time I just don't get it.

8. I love Jesus with all of my heart, but I want to love him better.

9. I am the unwitting serial killer of all houseplants. Apparently, I don't discriminate.

10. I cry when I'm mad but rarely when I'm sad.

11. I can pretty much sing any commercial jingle from my childhood up until now.

12. If I had the nerve I would get my nose pierced.

13. When I'm introduced to someone I never listen to their name, but I will never forget their face.

14. I am so humbled that God has allowed me to be the mother of four of the most beautiful people I have ever met.

15. I was engaged at age 16 and have been married to the love of my life for the last 27 years.

16. I was raised in a big city in Southern California and moved to a small town in North Carolina sixteen years ago.

17. I believe in the sanctity of human life so much that I will probably fight for the unborn until the day I die.

18. I can strike up a conversation with almost anyone— Once I chatted with the 411 operator for 18 minutes.

19. When a terrible storm is heading to my area I act real concerned like everyone else, but secretly I'm excited.

20. I feel exceedingly blessed in everything that matters most in life.

Schedule Traci Lester for a Speaking Event
tracilester@charter.net

Check out Traci's Blog at
teachingthebirdsandbees.com

11180223R00074

Made in the USA
San Bernardino, CA
08 May 2014